LYIN' EYES

JULIE MULHERN

J & M PRESS

❀ Created with Vellum

CHAPTER ONE

May, 1975
Kansas City, Missouri

I rested the box filled with my late husband's belongings on my hip and used my free hand to open the thrift shop door. "Rose, it's Ellison Russell. I'm back with the second load."

In a surge of pre-wedding nerves, I'd collected things I'd been meaning to get rid of for months—stray golf clubs, an ancient tennis racket, sweaters and shirts and shoes I'd missed on my first purge, books, a cummerbund set still new in its box, cufflinks, pocket squares, and the bedspread from the guest room where Henry slept the last year of our marriage—and packed them into boxes. There'd been so many unwanted items, my TR6 overflowed. Delivering Henry's stuff to the thrift shop required two trips.

"Thanks for staying late," I called. It was five o'clock, and by rights the shop manager should be on her way home. She'd agreed to stay while I fetched the boxes I couldn't fit in the car on my first trip. I hurried inside, maneuvered around a hanging rack filled with last year's styles, bumped my hip against a counter, and put the unwieldy box on a large table. Beyond the table, additional hanging racks stretched to the far wall. The clothes were organized by gender, age, and season. There was no point putting out Shetland sweaters in May or swimsuits in November. The thrift shop took donations and held them until the season they were most likely to sell. "There's one more box in the car, then I'm done."

I carried the second box inside, put it next to the first one, and called, "Rose?"

When she didn't answer, I pushed aside the curtain that separated the back room from the shop. "Rose?"

The sickly fluorescent bulbs that usually lit the store were off, but sunlight filtered past the dated mannequins posed in the plate-glass windows.

Where was Rose? She'd run the thrift shop for decades and treated the place like her second home. There were those who'd argue she treated the place like a fiefdom with herself as a despotic overlord. Either way, she'd never leave the back door unlocked and the store empty. A golf-ball-sized lump of dread rose from my stomach and lodged in my throat. I ventured onto the sales floor.

That's when I saw sensible rubber-soled shoes with their toes pointed upward. That's when I noticed the metallic tang of blood in the air.

Rose's body slotted between two racks of women's blouses. Her eyes stared sightlessly at the acoustical tile ceiling, and even in the dim light I could see the red dot that bloomed on her forehead.

I gasped, stumbled backward, and sent a display of used handbags crashing to the floor.

Oh dear Lord. Not only had I found a body, I'd disturbed a

crime scene. I turned, ready, willing, and able to pick up my mess before I called the police, but the second body froze my limbs. Another woman. This one collapsed between racks of men's shirts. Unlike Rose, her death wasn't clean. Someone had beaten her so brutally I couldn't make out her features.

I pressed a hand to my mouth and screwed my eyes shut, hoping the dead women might disappear.

I peeked.

Nope. Still there. Worse, I noticed an additional detail. Whoever had beaten the woman to death had used my late husband's pitching wedge.

I retreated to the stock room, snatched up the phone, took a few seconds to forcefully swallow the golf ball of dread, and dialed my fiancé, Detective Anarchy Jones. When he answered, I couldn't speak. "*Eep*."

"Ellison? Are you alright? What's happened?" Hearing his voice made things both better and worse. Better, because he'd take charge; worse, because our wedding was three days away and I'd just involved him in a murder investigation. Strictly speaking, Anarchy wasn't on duty. He was supposed to be recuperating from a gunshot wound. Instead, he was climbing the walls.

"You're not going to believe this," I whispered. "But I found..."

"You didn't." He knew my propensity for finding bodies.

My lips felt numb, and speaking came hard. "I did."

"Are you hurt? Are you safe?"

"No and yes."

"Where are you?"

"The Junior League Thrift Shop."

"You're kidding."

"I wish I was."

"Who?"

"The manager, Rose Reynolds, and someone else."

"I'll call Peters, then I'm on my way." He sounded almost chipper, as if a double homicide was just the distraction he needed. "You're sure you're safe?"

The store felt empty, and I didn't sense a threat. "I'll wait in the back lot." What if I was wrong? Had the two dead women sensed they had only moments to live? "Actually, I'll move my car to the front of the store and wait there." Where steady traffic provided plenty of witnesses. "See you soon." I didn't add, *please hurry*, but I bet he heard it in my voice.

Anarchy arrived seven long minutes later, and I fell into his arms. He stroked my hair and made soothing noises, and some of the tightness in my chest eased. I might have stayed like that forever, but other cars arrived, including one carrying Anarchy's partner.

Detective Peters made Peter Falk's Columbo look like a neat freak. He was gruff, irascible, slept in his raincoat, and only tolerated me to keep peace with Anarchy. He grunted. "What we got?"

Reluctantly, I separated from Anarchy's chest. "Two dead women."

"You're finding them in multiples now?"

I ignored his jibe. "One of them is Rose Reynolds. She's the store manager."

"Do you know the other one?" asked Anarchy.

The golf ball made a reappearance in my throat, and my eyes welled. That poor woman; whoever killed her made sure she suffered. "I couldn't tell."

Anarchy reached for my hand and squeezed.

"This isn't the kind of place you shop," said Peters. "Not la-di-da enough. What are you doing here?"

I ignored the la-di-da comment and said, "Donating some of my late husband's things." I glanced at Anarchy, who watched me with worried coffee-brown eyes. "I cleaned out closets for you."

His grip on my hand tightened.

"So you walked in and found them?" asked Peters.

"I put a box on the table in the back. When Rose didn't answer my call, I went looking for her. She's been shot."

"And the other woman?" asked Anarchy.

I stared into his eyes. "Beaten to death with Henry's nine iron. My prints will be all over it."

"You said you brought a box." Peters' tone was accusing.

"The box was part of the second load. The first trip I brought sporting goods and the bedspread from one of the guest rooms."

"You were here twice?" The glint in Anarchy's eyes said he was already creating a timeline.

"I arrived around four fifteen and dropped off the first load. I was here for twenty minutes, then I went home to pick up the rest."

"Who was here when you left?" asked Peters.

"Rose and a customer. A woman." I closed my eyes and remembered the young woman who'd perused a rack of dresses. "She looked familiar, but I can't place her."

"Is she the dead woman?"

I pictured her. Pretty, with a pert nose and long brown hair. She'd worn a peasant blouse and jeans. The dead woman wore a skirt. "No. Not unless she changed her clothes."

"What time did you arrive with your second load?" asked Anarchy.

"A few minutes before five."

"We have less than thirty minutes as a window." Anarchy inclined his head toward the door.

Peters grumbled and pulled on the handle. "It's locked."

"They take donations at the back door. That's how I got in."

Peters scowled at me.

The scowl was unwarranted. First off, I hadn't locked the door. Secondly, the thrift shop sat at the end of a strip mall. If Peters walked around the side of the building, he'd be inside.

And frankly, the man had put on a few pounds. Walking wouldn't hurt him one little bit.

He trudged out of sight, and a moment later he unlocked the front door and stared at Anarchy. "Jones, you'd better see this."

Anarchy lingered next to me. "You're okay?"

"I'm fine. The handbags on the floor—" I waved toward the shop "—are my fault. I knocked over the rack."

He waited for more.

"I bumped into the rack backing away from a body. If you don't need me, I'll go home."

"You're okay to drive?"

My insides wobbled like Jell-O, but I kept my voice steady. "I am. You know where to find me."

He kissed my cheek and whispered, "Love you."

Anarchy, who had no business investigating a murder this week, disappeared into the shop, and I got in my car and drove home.

I parked in front of the house and sat in the car without moving. My thoughts were a jumble, and I rested my head against the seat back and squeezed my eyes shut. Part of me mourned the dead women—they'd lost their lives, they deserved justice. Another more selfish part screamed *why me?* What karmic scale had I tipped to become a body magnet? And how could I adjust the weights so someone else found the bodies?

No answers presented themselves, so I climbed out of the car and went inside. Max, my Weimaraner with plans for world domination, met me at the front door. I crouched and scratched behind his ears. He wagged his approval, then rubbed his head against me, his version of a doggy hug.

"Thanks," I told him. "I needed that."

Together we headed to the kitchen, where Aggie, my housekeeper, was cooking. Whatever it was smelled amazing. She looked up from the stove when Max and I entered.

"Smells good." I crossed to the refrigerator, selected a battle of wine, and poured myself an extra-large glass.

Aggie's brows lifted. "Problem?"

"Two of them."

Now her brow wrinkled. "They wouldn't take your donation?"

"I found two bodies."

Aggie put down her spatula and stared. "At the thrift shop?"

I nodded.

"Hold on." She removed the pan from the heat and turned off the burner. "What happened?"

I told her.

She winced when I told her about Rose, and her eyes widened when I recounted the second woman's injuries.

I took a large sip of wine. "Why were they killed different ways?" The question wasn't rhetorical. Aggie's late husband was a private investigator, and she'd assisted with his cases. With her sproingy red hair and penchant for brightly colored muumuus (today she wore a ruffled red bandana apron over a lime muumuu splashed with orange flowers—the artist in me cringed), Aggie might look like a mild eccentric, but she possessed sharp intelligence and street sense.

"My guess? The unknown woman was the target, and the manager was collateral. Beating someone like that speaks of violent anger."

"As opposed to shooting them?"

"Which death would you prefer?"

"Fair point."

Brnng, brnng.

We both gazed at the phone.

"What are the chances that's Mother?" To say my mother, Frances Walford, disapproved of her daughter finding bodies was like saying Peter Rodino disapproved of Nixon. To wit, an understatement of epic proportions.

Brnng, brnng

"Did you see anyone you know at the crime scene?"

"Just Anarchy and Peters."

"She can't know. Not yet."

I didn't share Aggie's optimism. Mother had psychic powers when it came to her daughters. I tamped down a sigh and picked up the receiver. "Russell residence."

"Mom?" The voice was far too youthful to belong to Mother.

"It's Grace," I told Aggie.

"I'm going to miss dinner," said my daughter. "Debbie and I haven't finished working on our history project." The school year was almost over, and completing end-of-the-year projects and studying for finals were keeping Grace busy.

"What time will you be home?" My response was automatic.

"Nine."

"Fine. See you then." I hung up the phone and collapsed onto the nearest stool. "Grace won't be home for dinner." I glanced at the clock on the wall and winced. "Sorry she'd didn't call earlier."

"We're having French bread pizza tonight."

I shifted my gaze to the pan on the stove. "What's that?" French bread pizza required only a hot oven.

"Prep for hors d'oeuvres for this weekend." Aggie's face clouded. "Will these murders affect the wedding?"

The florist was set to arrive at eight in the morning. Tomorrow they'd bring potted plants, string lights, and begin the three day process of transforming my home and patio.

"Peters can investigate without Anarchy." That was true. Also true? Anarchy had a difficult time leaving investigations at the station. He'd ponder who'd killed those women right up to the moment he said, "I do."

Brnng, brnng.

Aggie wiped her hands on her apron. "I'll get it. Russell residence." She listened and gave me a thumbs up. Whoever was on the line wasn't Mother. "She's right here." She held out the phone and whispered, "Libba."

I lifted the receiver to my ear. "Hello."

"I'm picking you up at eleven tomorrow." Libba and our friends Jinx and Daisy were hosting a luncheon for me at the club.

"I'll be ready."

"Good. Is Anarchy there?"

"Not at the moment." I didn't add that he was investigating a murder when he should be resting.

"You're sure you don't mind if I bring Charlie to the wedding?" Charlie was my first love, my new next-door neighbor, and Libba's current beau.

"Why would I mind?"

"You have a history."

"That was high school."

"I don't want to make things awkward."

"They won't be."

She exhaled.

"You like him," I observed. "A lot."

"What if I do?"

"You're sure? He's age appropriate." Libba's last boyfriend was fifteen years younger. "He wears men's clothes." Libba had dated a cross-dresser. "And he hasn't murdered anyone."

"Very funny," said my best friend. "It's not as if your first pick was a prince."

That was a direct hit. Henry had cheated on me with reckless abandon, and that was the least of his sins. "Second time's a charm."

"After all those years with Henry, you deserve a man who treats you the way Anarchy does."

Sometimes it seemed too good to be true—too good to last. I crossed my fingers. "Thank you."

"Ellison!" Mother's voice carried from the foyer.

My shoulders tensed. "Libba, Mother's here. I'll see you tomorrow."

We hung up, and I braced myself. If Mother had heard I'd found two bodies, she'd have a how-could-you lecture prepared (she didn't grasp that I didn't find bodies on purpose). If it wasn't the why-does-my-daughter-find-dead-people lecture, she'd thought of yet another reason to postpone the wedding.

"In the kitchen," I called.

Seconds later she appeared. She wore a spring suit in a delicate celadon. Her makeup was restrained, and her hair formed a perfect silver helmet. She offered Aggie a regal nod, then fixed a gimlet eye on me. "We need to talk."

Oh, joy. "Of course. Let me refill my wine." I suspected I was going to need it.

"Aggie, a gin and tonic, please?" She peered out the window. "It's a lovely evening. We'll have drinks on the patio."

"Mother."

She lifted a questioning brow.

"This is my house."

"Your point, dear?"

If I ground my teeth any harder, I'd need to find time for a trip to the dentist.

Max took the room's temperature and slinked away.

Aggie presented Mother with her cocktail.

She frowned. "No lime?"

"We're out," I snapped.

"You're very testy."

Finding bodies did that to me. That and Mother's high-handedness. "What may I help you with, Mother?"

Mother breezed onto the patio and took a seat. "It occurred to me, you should amend your will." She perched on the edge of a wrought-iron chair with her ankles crossed and the gin and tonic cradled in her hands. "In case something happens to you. You do want your money to go to Grace, don't you?"

"What I do with my money is not your concern."

"Don't be naïve."

"Mother—" I put my wine glass on the side table and clasped my hands tightly "—I'm going to pretend you didn't start this conversation."

"I'm looking out for your best interests. And Grace's."

"Anarchy is not some gold-digger trying to steal my child's inheritance."

She winced. "I didn't say that."

"You came close."

"Ellison, we've seen this happen too often. There's a second wife and all of a sudden, children from the first marriage are cut out."

I stood. "Thank you for your concern." I walked to the back door and opened it.

"Where are you going?"

"Inside."

"I'm not done talking."

I managed a chilly smile. "But I'm done listening. I look forward to seeing you at the wedding."

I hurried into the kitchen and hit a solid chest. "*Oomph*."

Gentle hands circled my arms. "Are you okay?"

I looked over my shoulder at Mother who seethed on the patio.

Anarchy followed my gaze and offered me a sympathetic grimace (his mother wasn't easy either).

"I didn't expect to see you so soon," I said.

"We identified the second body."

"Who is it?"

"Her name is Avery Stallard. Do you know her?"

My lungs deflated. "Yes."

I glanced again at Mother. Was she psychic with her gold-digger talk? I leaned against the counter and swallowed a sigh. "Avery married Geoffrey Stallard about a year ago. She's thirty years younger than her husband. His children hate her." Hate was too weak a word. They despised her with the searing intensity of the sun's surface.

"How many children?"

"Four."

"You know them?"

"Some better than others. Their names are Dorothea, she goes by Dot, Victoria, her nickname is Tori, James, and Paige."

Mother stepped inside, and Anarchy smiled warmly. "Good evening, Frances."

"Good evening." She looked down her nose. "Done for the day?"

"No." Regret colored his tone. "But I had a question about one of the victims."

"Victims?"

Ix-nay on the urder-may alk-tay. I dragged a finger across my throat, but Anarchy, who was still smiling at Mother, didn't see me.

"At the thrift shop," Anarchy supplied.

"Oh?" Mother's eyes narrowed. "Victims at the thrift shop? Who found the bodies?"

Too late, Anarchy realized his mistake and gave me a panicked look. But we'd gone too far. There was nothing he could do to save us.

"I did. I found them."

Mother's lips disappeared in a thin line, and she turned toward me. "You forgot to mention that."

"Did I? An oversight."

"I'm sure." Her voice was desert dry. "Who died?

"Rose, the thrift-shop manager, and Avery Stallard."

"Horrible woman," said Mother.

"Rose or Avery Stallard?" asked Anarchy.

"The Stallard woman." Mother and Geoffrey Stallard's first wife, Ellen, had been close friends. When Ellen died from cancer, Mother mourned with her friend's husband. Later, Mother and her set had thinned their lips and lifted their noses when he took up with Avery. "She married for money, and look what it got her."

Oh. Dear. Lord. Marrying for money as justification for murder?

"Mother was just leaving."

Mother didn't budge. Instead, a calculating gleam lit her eyes. "You're investigating? Should you postpone the wedding?"

Anarchy pulled me close, and the look he gave Mother was mild. "Peters is the lead detective. We're not postponing. We look forward to celebrating with you."

Mother ceded with a nod, but I wasn't fooled. She wouldn't give up on driving a wedge between Anarchy and me until the minister declared us man and wife—and maybe not then.

CHAPTER TWO

I climbed into Libba's red Mercedes convertible and smoothed my skirt over my knees. The yellow of my dress was as springy as daffodils, and I allowed myself a moment's self-congratulation. It was the perfect frock for a May luncheon.

Libba paused with her fingers on the driver's door handle. "You found Avery Stallard?"

News traveled fast. "Can we not talk about murder?"

"Fine. But tell me one thing. Does Frances know?"

"Yes."

Libba winced on my behalf. "At least you're not a suspect." She slid behind the wheel. "Are you?"

"No."

"Pays to sleep with a cop." She put the car in gear, raced down the drive, and turned right without checking traffic.

I didn't need to sleep with a cop to avoid being a suspect. I was innocent. But Libba swerved, and fear kept me from pointing that out. I repressed the urge to clutch the dashboard. Instead, I squeezed my eyes shut and said a silent prayer.

The drive to the country club was especially short since we

nearly broke the sound barrier. Somehow we arrived without maiming or killing anyone. I counted that as a miracle and whispered my thanks to God.

Libba hopped out of the car and opened the trunk.

"What's that?" I nodded at the large beautifully wrapped gift (shiny white paper, enormous white satin bow) she now held. "Is this a shower? You promised no gifts."

She shrugged. "I lied."

"I don't need anything."

"A, when has that ever stopped you? B, yes, you do."

"What do I need?"

A cat-that-swallowed-the-canary smile spread across her face. "When was the last time you bought lingerie to please a man?"

My mouth opened and closed, but there were no words. She'd rendered me mute.

"That's what I thought." That smirk of hers was incredibly annoying. I'd tell her that as soon as I regained rudimentary communication skills.

For now, I imagined box after box of sexy underwear piled in front of me while golfers and bridge players peeked into the dining room to see who was having a party. I blushed in anticipation. No wonder Libba insisted on driving me here. If I had a car, I'd leave.

"Stop scowling," she said. "It will give you wrinkles. Besides, you'll have a marvelous time. I promise."

I had my doubts, but I followed her inside.

"Is that Dot Thompson?" Libba pointed. "Down the hall talking to the event manager."

Dot Thompson, née Stallard, didn't notice us.

"Do you think she's planning a the-witch-is-dead party?" asked Libba.

"The reception after the funeral." My words were back!

"Pooh." Libba wrinkled her nose. "My idea sounds like more fun."

"If you ask me, it's the same party." Anarchy would consider Geoffrey Stallard's children persons of interest in Avery's murder. For Dot's sake, I hoped she hadn't booked a marching band, balloons, and confetti.

Our steps brought us closer to her, and she glanced at us and froze. "Ellison."

We exchanged a quick hug.

"Dot." I couldn't say I was sorry for her loss. Not when she'd once called Avery a black-hearted, gold-digging tramp who was erasing Ellen Stallard's memory. "How's your father?"

"He's holding up. Thank you for asking. I heard you found her."

The memory of her brutalized corpse had me pulling breath deep into my lungs. "I did."

"How awful for you. And poor Rose. She was such a nice woman, and so near retirement."

"As much as Rose loved that place—" Libba held out her right hand and inspected her manicure "—she probably didn't mind dying there."

Dot and I stared at her with open mouths. I remembered Mother's warning about flies and closed mine.

"What?" Libba dropped her hand and frowned at us. "The woman might as well have slept on a cot in the stock room. Name me one time in our adult lives when you've been at the thrift shop when Rose wasn't there." When neither Dot nor I responded, Libba nodded as if we'd proved her point. "I'm not saying her death is a good thing, only that if she could have picked the place, she'd have picked that shop."

Dot nodded. "You might be right."

"Of course I'm right."

This conversation was unutterably sad. "When is Avery's service?" I asked.

"Next Tuesday." Dot side-eyed the event manager. "I'd like to do it sooner." She bit each word as if the sooner Avery Stallard was in the ground, the better. "But the club is closed on Mondays."

"I'll be out of town, but I'll be thinking of you." We all knew that was a whopper. I'd be on my honeymoon and wouldn't waste a thought for friends who didn't mourn their stepmother's passing. "Aggie baked a Bundt. Should I take it by your father's house?"

"Chocolate?" An avaricious gleam flickered in Dot's eyes.

"Yes."

"When are you bringing it?"

"This afternoon?"

Dot's wrinkled forehead suggested she was mentally reorganizing her day. "I suppose Dad's house would be best. Thank you, Ellison."

"Aggie does bake a delicious cake," said Libba. "Too bad someone has to die to get one."

I gaped at my too-blunt friend, but Dot nodded as if she were happy to make the trade. "I won't keep you."

Libba nodded and pulled me toward a private dining room with a golf-course view.

Six tables were set with cloths as verdantly green as the grass outside. Bright flowers rioted in silver Revere bowls—hyacinths and lilies and lilacs and hydrangeas.

Six tables? "Libba, it's beautiful. Thank you."

"I hear a 'but' coming."

"You said this was a small luncheon."

"You have loads of friends who knew Henry. Now that you've found someone better, they want to wish you happiness."

My heart (and throat) swelled.

Libba cut her gaze at me. "Don't cry. You'll smear your makeup." She waved at a waitress. "Two mimosas, please."

I swallowed my emotions and patted under my eyes. "The flowers are spectacular."

"The florist is coming back this afternoon. He'll take the bouquets to the Alameda for your out-of-town guests."

"That's so thoughtful. Thank you." I accepted a Champagne flute from the waitress.

"I can be thoughtful. You don't have to sound surprised."

"I'm not remotely surprised." I lifted my mimosa. "To best friends."

She clinked her glass against mine. "Forever."

Jinx and Daisy arrived with Pam Ellis in tow. They all deposited beautifully wrapped packages on the gift table before walking toward Libba and me.

We kissed. We hugged. We exclaimed over each other's dresses. And when we were done, Jinx fixed her gaze on me and asked, "Is it true? Did you find Avery Stallard's body?"

"And Rose Reynolds'. I'll tell you later." No murder talk, not at this luncheon. I turned to Pam. "It's such a treat to see you. Catch me up on your children."

Pam and I had been friends since grade school, but our paths seldom crossed. Our children attended different schools, we belonged to different country clubs, and we volunteered for different organizations. Even at the League, we sat on different committees.

"Wilton will be a high-school freshman in the fall."

"Already? How is that possible? I'm sure he's excited. What's he doing this summer?"

"Swim team, golf, tennis, and mowing lawns."

"Busy summer," I observed. "What about Annie?"

"Much the same, without the lawns. We leave for Harbor Point after swim champs and won't come back till school starts."

"How divine."

"You and your new husband should visit."

"We'd love that, but I have a full summer ahead of me."

"Oh?"

"I'm helping with swim team, I have a gallery opening in the fall, and—"

"And a new husband you're not ready to share. When things settle down, you must visit. Next summer. How's Grace?

"Fabulous. Like your children, she has swim team, golf, and tennis, plus she'll babysit quite a bit."

"So good for the kids to earn their own money. If they don't, how will they know what a dollar's worth?"

To my knowledge, Pam had never held a paying job, not even as a babysitter. "You're so right."

She glanced at the rapidly filling room. "I won't monopolize your time, but may I call you? I was on the League's thrift-shop committee."

She wanted to hear about poor Rose. "Of course."

She stepped aside, and Laura Gilchrist took her place. I welcomed her with a smile, spotted unexpected guests over her shoulder, and felt my face go slack. Aunt Sis, my half-sister Karma, and Mother stood at the room's entrance.

Mother? At a lingerie shower? Since Libba was a hostess, I could guarantee naughty underwear. I blinked rapidly—just to make sure I wasn't hallucinating. Nope. Mother, wearing a Chanel suit, a rope of pearls, and a pinched expression, was still framed by the entrance. I resisted burying my head in my hands.

Mother would get her wish. There'd be no wedding. Because I was going to jail for murdering Libba. My gaze sought my former best friend.

She offered me a what-was-I-supposed-to-do shrug and mouthed, "Frances."

Mother had railroaded her?

That I believed. Mother could roll over the First Infantry Division without breaking a sweat. But a little warning?

Laura turned her head and paled. "I didn't realize your mother was coming."

I'd only thought of myself when I saw Mother. But what of the guests? Mother would judge each peignoir, each teddy, each garter belt.

"I didn't realize either. Would you please excuse me?" I approached my family. "Karma, Aunt Sis, what a wonderful surprise."

After a flurry of hugs, I turned to Mother. "Good morning."

She eyed the overflowing gift table.

"I told Libba no gifts." I sounded defensive. I couldn't help it.

"*Hmph*. By now you should know she doesn't listen to you."

"Ellison, your glass is empty." Karma took my elbow and led me to the bar. "Two mimosas." When the bartender served our drinks, she nodded her thanks. "You didn't know we were coming?"

"I thought you were arriving late this afternoon, but I'm thrilled you're here."

"And Frances?"

I drained the flute and presented it to the bartender for a refill. There was only one way to survive this luncheon, and it included lots more Champagne.

The room filled. Ladies chatted and tittered and drank mimosas. At five minutes till noon, Libba tinged a silver spoon against a Champagne flute. "Everyone, please take your seats."

Someone, probably Daisy, had taken the trouble to make place cards. I found myself seated between Jinx and Karma at a table that also included Mother, Aunt Sis, Pam Ellis, Laura Gilchrist, and Sydney Barnes.

Sydney leaned over her cream of artichoke soup and said, "I heard what happened. How perfectly awful for you."

Mother's sharp intake of breath was a warning unheeded.

Sydney was a lovely woman with golden blonde hair, blue eyes, and a near-constant smile. That smile and a refreshing naivete had won over doubters when she married Mark, a man fourteen years her senior. "Rose was such a sweet woman," she continued. "I can't imagine anyone killing her."

No one stated the obvious. Avery was the target.

Sydney downed half a mimosa in one sip. "Maybe she got caught in Avery's murder."

No one said "duh." I thought it showed great restraint.

"Do you think her husband did it?" she asked.

"Geoffrey? A killer?" Mother sounded affronted. "Why would you suggest such a thing?"

"Isn't the spouse usually guilty?"

Jinx choked on her sparkling water and cut her eyes at me. "Not always."

"But Avery was having an affair." Sydney had our undivided attention now. No one said a word as the waiters cleared empty soup cups and served crab imperial.

"How do you know?" Jinx never accepted unsubstantiated gossip.

"I saw her coming out of a hotel room with a man who wasn't Geoffrey." She took a sip of her mimosa. "Like Geoffrey, but thirty years too young. It was obvious what they'd been doing. She saw me and begged me not to tell."

The silence at our table was deafening.

"But now that she's dead, I can tell you."

"What were you doing at a hotel?" asked Mother.

"Me?" Sydney wrinkled her nose. "When Mark and I are feeling stale, we sneak off to a hotel for a little afternoon delight."

Mother choked on her drink. She did not hold Sydney (or any much-younger wife) in high esteem. She'd watched too many husbands swap their first wives, women rounded by age and children and summers spent in the sun, for nubile second wives. And she did not approve. For her, hearing about Sydney's sex life was beyond the pale.

"What did Avery say when you saw her?" Pam filled the uncomfortable silence.

"She explained she wasn't emotionally cheating. She swore she loved Geoffrey, but she was having trouble getting pregnant."

We stared slack jawed.

"Are you telling us Avery Stallard stood in a hotel corridor and told you she was trying to get pregnant with another man's baby and pass the child off as her husband's?" Mother usually saved that chilly tone for me—when I told her I'd found a body.

"It sounds awful when you say it that way."

"How else would one say such a thing?" Smoke rose from Mother's nose.

"She didn't tell me while we were at the hotel," Sydney explained. "We met for a glass of wine. She wanted a baby, and her husband couldn't give her one."

"Was Geoffrey aware of her...efforts?" asked Pam.

Sydney frowned. "I don't think so."

"Who was the man?" I asked.

"I didn't get his name, but..."

"But?"

"Like I said, he looked like Geoffrey."

"No wonder the woman was murdered," said Aunt Sis. "Ellison, have I told you about our recent trip to Hong Kong?"

The waiters appeared with the next course, smoked chicken served over bibb lettuce with fresh berries on the side, and Aunt Sis regaled the table with tales of Orient.

Twenty minutes later, the waiter placed a maple mousse topped with rum sauce in front of me, and I lifted my spoon.

"Save it for later," said Libba, who'd positioned herself near my chair. "It's time to open your gifts."

I stood and whispered, "Have you lost your mind?"

"What do you mean?"

"Mother's here."

"She knows about sex, Ellison. She had it at least twice."

"I'm not worried about Mother." Half the women at the luncheon were squirming in their seats in anticipation of Frances Walford's judgmental stare. "I'm worried about our friends."

She frowned and scanned the tables filled with nervous women. "Oh."

"That's all you have to say?"

"Whoops?"

Oh dear Lord.

I returned to our table and forced a polite smile. "Mother, may I see you in the hallway?"

She gave a regal nod, stood, and followed me into the hall. "What is it, Ellison?"

"I didn't anticipate gifts."

She inclined her head, a queen listening to a slow-witted subject blather. "As you told me."

"The guests—" I gazed first at the ceiling, then the carpet beneath our feet "—I don't think they anticipated your presence."

"Are you suggesting they gave you scandalous lingerie?" She lifted a single brow. "Lingerie they'd rather I not see?"

"It's possible."

She nodded. Slowly. "You will open my gift and Sis's, then we'll leave."

"Thank you."

"And you'll return the scandalous lingerie."

"None of your business, Mother."

She sighed as if I were a great trial. "Let's get this over with."

We returned to the dining room, where the guests had surrounded Aunt Sis. Not surprising. Aunt Sis was great fun. She'd led an unconventional life and possessed a repertoire of fabulous stories. She leaned forward as if she were imparting a state secret. "Frances met him at the door wearing nothing but the frilly apron. Only problem? It wasn't Harrington. It was the milkman who'd forgotten to include the butter in her order."

The room erupted in laughter, and Mother hissed. A full-on pit viper hiss. "Sis!"

Sis didn't hear her. She was too busy laughing with the women gathered around her.

"Is that true?" I covered my mouth and hid the smile that might get me gutted.

"I'll deal with your aunt later." Mother, who'd possessed the foresight to bring her handbag into the hallway, turned on her heel and left.

Not good. I didn't want Aunt Sis and Mother at each other's throats at my wedding. When they were mad, they were so cold to each other the temperature fell to freeze-Acapulco levels. I'd need a fur coat to walk down the aisle. I almost went after Mother. But what could I say? Aunt Sis didn't mean it? Of all the stories she could tell, Sis chose one that put Mother in a ridiculous light. Probably to put the other guests at ease. But Mother, who didn't enjoy laughing at herself, wouldn't see it that way. She'd see it as mockery, and betrayal, and meriting a beheading.

"There's the bride," called Libba.

I gave myself a few seconds to gather my courage (Mother and I were in accord on laughing at ourselves), slapped on a bright smile, and returned to my party.

"Sit," Libba instructed. "Open this one first." She handed me the white-on-white package, and her eyes twinkled with naughty delight.

The diaphanous gown inside the box was nearly see-through.

I blushed a deep crimson, and Libba cackled. "Give me that bow." She collected the satin ribbon from my lap and said, "Anarchy will love you in that."

If I ever found the courage to wear it.

CHAPTER THREE

I stood in Geoffrey Stallard's foyer and gaped.

Tori Parks (Geoffrey's second daughter) offered me a wry smile. "Everyone who walks in has the same reaction."

"It's so different." The last time I visited the Stallard home, antiques and oriental rugs harmonized with the stately Tudor's classic architecture. The antiques were gone, replaced by modern furniture. The Heriz and Kirman rugs Ellen Stallard adored had disappeared. Instead, my feet sank into ankle-deep shag carpet.

"Avery would have moved if she could, but Dad refused to sell the house. This—" she waved at the harvest-gold grass-cloth wallpaper "—cost a fortune."

"Did she use a decorator?"

Tori rolled her eyes. "She did. Can you believe it? I'm grateful Dad wouldn't let her sell Mom's furniture or rugs. Everything is in storage. If he wants the house the way it should be, he can move it back."

"So glad that's an option."

"Speaking of Mom's things, did you see what Avery took to the thrift shop?"

"I'm sorry, no."

She gave a discouraged sigh. "We just discovered Mom's tea towels are gone. It's a little thing, but Mom stitched them when she was a girl with her grandmother. It's how she learned to sew. I hate to think Avery gave them away."

"She didn't call and ask if you wanted them?"

Something ugly flashed across Tori's face. "No, she did not."

I closed my eyes and pictured the stock room. "Honestly, I didn't notice. Pam Ellis is on the League's thrift-shop committee. I bet she'd have the staff look for them."

"That's a good idea. Thank you."

I held out Aggie's chocolate Bundt cake.

"This is so kind of you. With everything you have going on, you baked."

"I can't take credit. Aggie baked."

She accepted the cake. "Thank you."

"You're welcome. My life is a bit crazy right now, but if you or Dot need anything, I hope you'll call."

"We will. If you'd like to speak to Dad, he's in the living room." She headed to the dining room and added Aggie's Bundt to the food already crowding the table, and I stepped into the living room.

Geoffrey Stallard stood next to the fireplace and rested his hand on the mantle. His leonine hair was silver, but his brows were still dark. The man was famous for his year-round tan, but today his skin looked yellow, as if heartache gave him jaundice. His lips dragged down, and mist trailed across his gray eyes. Paige, his youngest daughter, stood next to him and smiled politely as Jane Addison offered condolences (or, more likely, offered her help in selling Geoffrey's house).

Laura Gilchrist joined me at the room's entrance. "Crowded place."

At least twenty or thirty people clustered in the living room, and there were more in the dining and family rooms. "It is."

"Finding them was so unlucky for you."

I could argue that Rose and Avery were the unlucky ones. Instead, I nodded.

"I dropped a box of Charles's things off last week. If I'd waited, it could have been me." She shuddered. "Who found them, I mean. I keep thinking about what Sydney said at lunch."

Now was neither the time nor the place to discuss Avery's extracurriculars. "I wish Syd had kept that secret." What good could come of everyone in town knowing Avery cheated on Geoffrey? And worse, with the goal of getting herself pregnant with another man's baby?

"Do you think it's true?" Laura whispered.

James Stallard's appearance saved me from answering. He kissed my cheek. "Ellison, it's nice of you to come. I'm told you found her."

"I did. I'm so sorry for your family's loss."

He winced and held out his hand to Laura. "James Stallard."

"Laura Gilchrist. Dot and I are friends." Dot, who was my age, and Tori had birthdays a year apart. There was a ten-year gap between the two sisters and James and Paige. The siblings weren't familiar with each other's friends.

"Thank you for coming, Laura." Unlike his sisters, James wasn't surrounded by an aura of barely contained glee, but he didn't strike me as grieving.

The front bell rang, and he shifted his gaze to the door. "If you'll excuse me, it's my turn."

Laura watched him go. "I heard he introduced Avery to Geoffrey."

That piqued my interest. "Did he?"

"He was dating her, and he brought her round to meet his father. She switched her affections."

Wow. "Was James furious?"

"He got over it. The girls blame him for bringing a viper into the nest."

"Do they?" I had more questions, but Paige Stallard caught my eye and waved me over.

"Excuse me, Laura." I approached Paige with trepidation. She had a colorful history. Her sisters attributed Paige's erratic behavior to diet pills. Yes, she was as slender as a reed, but the zesty living had started long before her doctor prescribed amphetamines to control her waistline.

She took my hands in hers and held fast. "You found the witch."

Next to her, Geoffrey winced.

When I was a child, forty seemed impossibly old, and sixty had seemed one step from crumbling to dust. Now that my fourth decade was tapping me on the shoulder, forty didn't seem old at all. And sixty? Who was to say sixty couldn't be vibrant? Geoffrey Stallard wore his sixties well. The man had to be sixty-five, and he looked young, virile, and sad.

"Mr. Stallard, I'm so sorry for your loss."

"Ellison, thank you for coming. And, please, 'Mr. Stallard' makes me feel ancient. Call me Geoffrey."

Now came the time for me to say something nice about the deceased. "Avery was a beautiful woman."

Next to her father, Paige snorted.

He frowned at her.

"Pretty is as pretty does," she muttered.

"Enough, Paige."

"Ellison found Avery's body."

The air around Geoffrey pulsed with emotion. His mouth worked, but he didn't speak. Long seconds stretched. "That must have been terrible for you."

Worse for Avery. "Again, I'm sorry for your loss." I didn't offer Paige my sympathies. Not only had she called Avery a witch, she looked ready to skip around a maypole.

I moved on so the next person could offer condolences, and

Jane Addison grabbed my arm. As a real estate agent, Jane made it her business to know gossip. After all, divorces and deaths meant listings. The couple whose last child was finishing college might downsize, and the newly engaged couple needed a place to lay their heads. But how could Avery's death could lead to a listing?

"You found her." Jane made finding a body sound like an accusation.

I grimaced. "Yes."

"I shouldn't speak ill of the dead, but—"

"Don't."

She blinked.

"Don't speak ill of her. She's been dead less than two days. You're in her house. Her husband—" who stood only ten feet from us "—is grieving. Don't do it." I'd heard nothing but horrible things about Avery Stallard. Horrible, terrible, petty things—but they didn't justify her violent death.

"Paige will get her inheritance now."

I blinked and tilted my head. Had I heard her correctly? "What?"

She screwed her face into a gotcha expression. "I thought you didn't want to hear ill of the dead?"

"What did Avery have to do with Paige's inheritance?"

"The terms of Ellen's will," she whispered. "The girls don't inherit until they're forty unless their father deems them responsible."

"Avery convinced Geoffrey that Paige couldn't handle the money?"

"I don't think it took much convincing."

Paige Stallard's fast-living reputation—liquor, pills, men—had come home to roost. And Jane's interest was suddenly obvious; Paige might soon have the means to buy a house.

"How did you hear about this?" I asked.

"This way." Jane led me into the dining room, where Dot

claimed the last slice of Aggie's cake, lifted the empty platter from the table, and disappeared through the kitchen door.

"Drat." Jane frowned her disappointment. "Aggie could sell those cakes, go into business."

"I'll tell her you said so. About the will?"

"A little bird told me." Her gaze scanned the dining room, stopping briefly Prudence Davies, a woman who'd had an affair with my late husband, and Lilly Frasier.

Two women I avoided whenever possible. I edged toward the door. "Birds can make mistakes."

"Not this one."

"Ellison." Mother's voice carried from the foyer.

I turned and forced a smile.

Jane abandoned me.

Mother sailed into the dining room. "I didn't expect to see you here."

Likewise. Mother wasn't remotely sorry Avery Stallard was dead, and to my knowledge, she hadn't spoken to Geoffrey since he married her.

"I brought a Bundt cake," I explained.

Her gaze shifted to the dining room table.

"It went fast."

She pursed her lips. "Your father's parking the car."

My father, Harrington Walford, and Geoffrey were golfing buddies, nineteenth-hole buddies, and poker buddies. All activities that did not include wives.

"It was kind of you to come."

Her pinched expression softened. "Geoffrey is a good man. He just fell for the wrong woman."

"He's grieving."

The pinched expression returned. "Men. It's always about proving their virility. How much money can they make? How many toys can they buy? How young is their wife?"

"Even Daddy?"

"Not your father." He wouldn't dare. "But otherwise. You can't deny I'm right."

"I won't argue your point." Speaking of arguing. "Did you talk to Sis?"

"I did not."

"She didn't mean to hurt your feelings."

"Did she think I'd be pleased she recounted that story?" Mother glanced around the dining room in case someone was listening. She spotted Prudence and her eyes narrowed.

"No one believed her."

Mother blinked.

"It was true?" That was a visual I didn't want.

"Sugar." Daddy's hug squeezed away the image of Mother in nothing but a frilly apron. "You ready for Saturday?"

"I am."

"You're glowing." He took Mother's hand. "She's glowing, Frannie."

"*Hmph.*"

"Where's Geoffrey?" he asked.

"Living room.

"I'll pay my respects. You coming, Frannie?"

Mother looked as if she'd rather take a girls' trip with Sydney, but she nodded. A slow, queenly nod. "Very well."

"We're meeting at the Alameda rooftop bar for cocktails at six. Can you come?" I asked.

"We?" asked Daddy.

"Gordon, Aunt Sis, and Karma." We'd made the arrangements before we left the shower. "I hope you'll join us."

Mother touched her hair near her temple. "I feel a headache coming on. We'll see you tomorrow."

She did not have a headache. She was mad at her sister. I offered her a tight smile. "I hope you feel better soon. Daddy, will you come? Karma would love to spend more time with you."

"Frannie, are you going home to rest?" His meaning was clear—he'd go without her.

"Perhaps if I take two aspirins I can muddle through."

"Wonderful." I offered her my best I-won-this-round smile. "I'll see you there."

GRACE FOLLOWED me to the Alameda. She needed her car in case drinks became dinner and dinner became a late night. With Aunt Sis and Gordon, a late night was a distinct possibility.

We rode the glass elevator to the rooftop bar.

"I bet this elevator is packed around Christmas." The hotel had a fabulous view of the Country Club Plaza.

"We'll do that this year. We'll have hot chocolate in the lounge, then ride this thing and admire the lights." Each holiday season, colored Christmas lights outlined the Plaza's Spanish architecture. The effect was magical.

"We can start a tradition. Maybe I'll do that with my kids." She side-eyed me. "Also, it's not too late. You and Anarchy could give me a sibling."

"No more kids for me. I have a perfect daughter. Why jeopardize my record?" Anarchy and I had talked about children, and he was fine with my decision not to have more.

The elevator arrived on the top floor, and we followed a piano's notes to the bar.

Karma had claimed a table near the window, and we joined her.

"Grace, you get prettier every time I see you."

Grace blushed at the compliment. "Thanks, Aunt Karma."

"How's school?"

"Almost over."

"I remember those days. Summer so close you can taste it, but exams and final papers in the way."

"It's worse when the weather is like this." Grace nodded toward the window and its view of a perfect spring evening.

Karma followed her gaze. "I have to know. Who paves a creek bed?" Brush Creek, which ran south of the Plaza, had been encased in concrete my whole life.

"A political boss with a concrete company. They say his enemies are buried underneath."

Karma grinned. "Always murder with you."

"Ellison, I want to hear more about the bodies." Aunt Sis had arrived.

Grace, Karma, and I stood, and Aunt Sis claimed hugs from each of us before she sank into a chair. "Sit next to me, dear." She smiled up at her husband, then shifted her gaze to me. "Sit. Tell us about the dead women."

"There's not much to tell. I walked into the thrift shop, found them, and called the police."

Aunt Sis caught a waiter's eye. "A bottle of Champagne." She glanced at Grace. "What would you like, dear?"

"A Tab, please. Two limes."

The waiter hurried to the bar, and Sis prompted, "There has to be more to the story." She rolled her hand in a start-talking gesture.

"Sis told me you found Geoffrey Stallard's second wife," said Gordon.

"And the thrift-shop manager. Her name was Rose Reynolds."

He rubbed his chin. "The Stallard woman was a piece of work."

No one had a kind word to say about her. "Geoffrey seems genuinely upset."

Gordon's salt and pepper brows rose. "When I talked to him two months ago, he told me he'd made a terrible mistake. Avery wanted a baby. Geoffrey didn't. Avery redid the house, and Geoffrey felt like a stranger in his own home. Geoffrey and

Ellen were a popular couple, but invitations to parties dried up when he married Avery."

Had Geoffrey faked his grief?

"Did he expect Ellen's friends to welcome her?" Aunt Sis smoothed her Thea Porter kaftan. "They were loyal to their friend and didn't want an example of trading in for a newer model flashed in their husbands' faces."

Gordon took Aunt Sis's hand and stared into her eyes. "That will never happen." He wore the besotted expression of a man hopelessly in love with his wife.

Grace, Karma, and I squirmed in our chairs.

"Is Anarchy coming?" asked Karma.

"If he can get away."

"What about Dad and Frances?"

"They should be here." I glanced at Aunt Sis, and she colored.

"Frannie may be a teensy bit miffed with me," she told her husband as she measured a tiny distance between her thumb and pointer finger.

Aunt Sis was the queen of understatement.

"In my defense, she told me that story so long ago, I forgot it was in confidence."

"What story?" asked Grace.

"Never mind." Karma, Aunt Sis, and I spoke as one.

"There's Frances," said Gordon.

"Not a word about Sis's story, Grace." Pursuing this topic around Mother would add gasoline to the fire. My expression communicated the dire consequences of disobedience.

She mouthed "later" and stood to welcome her grandparents.

Cheeks were kissed. Hands were clasped. Hugs were exchanged. The waiter appeared with Champagne.

"What are we celebrating?" asked Mother.

"Ellison's wedding," Aunt Sis replied.

"Oh. That."

"Do you need something stronger?" I asked sweetly. "A shot of bourbon?"

"Don't be ridiculous, Ellison. You know I drink scotch."

"Ellison was telling us about finding the bodies at the thrift shop," said Gordon. It was a heroic effort to cover our real topic of conversation, but it dropped me into the soup.

Mother looked at the waiter and said, "Make it a double."

Daddy chose to drink Champagne with the rest of us. "Where's Anarchy?"

"Working the case. I left a message for him. He'll join us if he can."

Daddy frowned. This was his fear for me—that I'd spend my married life waiting for a man more interested in avenging the dead than spending time with his wife.

Mother dug in her purse. "This came in the mail for you." She handed me an envelope. "Did you give them your actual address?"

"A million times." When my painting career took off and checks from galleries arrived on a regular basis, I expected Henry to be thrilled. He wasn't. I'd quietly redirected my business mail to my parents' home. Now that Henry was dead, there was one gallery that couldn't seem to make the address change.

"Open it," Mother instructed.

I slit the envelope, peeked inside, and added a trip to the bank to tomorrow's to-do list.

"Time for a toast," said Aunt Sis.

"Without me?"

I looked up at the man who'd joined us, and my heart skipped a beat. On Saturday, we'd exchange vows. He'd be my husband.

He bent and kissed my cheek.

"I'm glad you're here." I'd stolen Aunt Sis's queen-of-understatement crown. "Has Peters identified the killer?"

"Not yet."

Not surprising. More people wanted Avery dead than I could count on one hand, and they all had valid motives.

Silence fell as the waiter served drinks and fetched a Champagne flute for Anarchy.

When he left us, Mother squared her shoulders. "I'm quite sure the Stallard family is blameless."

Anarchy's expression was mild. "Oh?"

"They're a fine old family," Mother explained.

Members of fine old families committed murder. She knew that. She'd never admit that.

"Not one of them has an alibi," Anarchy replied.

Mother's sharp intake of breath cut through the room. She closed her eyes. "Paige," she ceded with a brief nod. "She's troubled."

That wasn't how murder worked. The killer was hardly ever the convenient suspect.

"Mother." Murder was messy. It involved innocent people—hurt innocent people. "Every member of that family had a reason to want her dead. Peters will investigate them. All of them."

She opened her eyes and glared at me. "Ellison, this is serious. You're friends with Dot and Tori. The Stallards won't forget your husband helped investigate them." She'd paled, a sure sign she was furious. "Do something, Harrington."

"Ellison's right, Frannie. The Stallards will be investigated. They're lucky Anarchy can run interference."

That wasn't what Anarchy did, but I wasn't about to correct Daddy. Not when he was on our side.

Aunt Sis cleared her throat. "About that toast." She lifted her glass. "To Ellison and Anarchy, we wish you every happiness."

We clinked our glasses, and Mother downed her scotch in one enormous swallow.

CHAPTER FOUR

I sat on the family room couch with Anarchy next to me. The weight of his arm across my shoulders felt right. Safe. Perfect. "You're a saint." No matter what Mother said, he was unfailingly polite while always taking my side.

He chuckled. "You mean Frances?"

"Who else?"

"My parents arrive tomorrow. We'll see who the saint is then."

Anarchy's parents. A chill skittered down my spine. The Joneses did not approve of Anarchy's choice. I suspected they used words like spoiled, entitled, and oblivious when they described me. For all her faults, Mother was a safer topic. "She truly believes the Stallards' blood is too blue for murder. You'd think she'd accept that anyone can be a killer." The rate at which I found bodies meant Mother knew killers. Lots of them.

"The Stallards are too posh for crime?" Anarchy knew better. He didn't expect an answer.

"What if Rose was the target?"

He considered the suggestion. "Maybe."

"I hear a 'but' coming."

"Rose had an easy death. The killer brutalized Avery. She suffered."

I focused on the ring on my left hand. It sparkled like crazy. I bit my lower lip.

"Something you want to tell me?"

Tori and Dot were dear friends, but Anarchy was more important to me. I let my hands fall to my lap. "There are things you should know."

"Have you been investigating?" He didn't say Peters would have my head, but it was implied.

"Me? No. Just listening."

"What did you hear?"

"Avery was cheating on Geoffrey with a younger man. She was trying to get pregnant. Also, according to Gordon, Geoffrey regretted marrying her."

"The man had a strong motive. What else?"

"Avery dated James Stallard before she married his father."

"Is there more?"

I stared at nothing, and said, "Tori and Dot hated her for attempting to erase their mother's memory."

"And Paige?"

"Avery convinced Geoffrey to withhold Paige's trust."

"Wow."

My sentiments exactly. Every member of the family had a reason to kill her.

"Did you hear anything about Rose?" he asked.

"She was dedicated to her job. That's it."

Anarchy pulled me closer.

"I'm taking a Bundt cake to Rose's sister tomorrow. Maybe I'll learn something then."

"What else are you doing tomorrow?"

"The florist has kicked me out of the house, so I'll run errands, have my nails done, and I might take my address book to the library or club and write thank-you notes."

"Thank-you notes? For what?"

"Didn't I tell you? The luncheon the girls hosted for me was a lingerie shower."

"Tell me more." He waggled his brows.

"I'd rather show you on our honeymoon." Worry nagged at me, and I asked, "You'll be able to leave, won't you?"

"Peters will handle the case." He didn't sound happy about it.

"Maybe you'll solve it before the wedding."

He glanced at his watch. "That's less than forty-eight hours." He kissed me. "In less than two days, you'll be my wife."

"I cleaned out a drawer for you."

"A whole drawer?"

"I created a foot of space in the walk-in closet."

"A whole foot?"

"It might be eleven inches." I snuggled closer. "All joking aside, I want this to be your home. We'll have the study painted."

"Henry's study?"

"Your study," I corrected. "What color would you like?"

"Surprise me."

"Plaid?" Wallpaper was a decent idea. "You wore a plaid jacket the morning I met you."

"And you wore a swimsuit and a man's dress shirt with a frayed collar. You were—you are—the most beautiful woman I've ever seen. Wherever you are is home."

Mother's opinions didn't matter. Neither did Anarchy's parents'. Not when the man next to me made my heart skip beats.

Woof! Max rested his chin on the sofa cushion and stared at us.

"He wants a walk."

"How can you tell?" Anarchy scratched behind Max's ears.

"That's his walk bark."

"Have you told him about McCallister?"

"Max, the cat is coming here to live."

Max growled.

"The two of you will not destroy the house."

Max met my gaze, but made no promises.

"Please?"

He blinked.

"I'll make it worth your while."

"Bribery?" asked Anarchy.

"For peace? You bet."

Woof.

"He wants that walk," I translated.

"Will he give up?"

"Never." I sighed.

"I'll go with you. Do you need to change?"

I wore the dress and pumps I'd put on this morning. "Give me five minutes."

I raced upstairs, threw on khakis, a light sweater, and a pair of Tretorns, then met Anarchy and Max at the front door.

Outside, the night was bathed in moonlight. Its silver drifted through the trees and across Anarchy's dark eyes. The flower-scented air was heavy with promise, and we moved closer together. Our lips inches apart.

Max nearly jerked my arm out of the socket.

"Max!" My scolding made not the slightest difference to him. There were night critters to catch, and he was the dog to catch them.

"You're sure we can't put him in the backyard?" The rough edge of Anarchy's voice promised toe-curling delights.

"If he messes up the florists' work, my name will be—what's worse than mud?"

"Dog doo?"

"My name will be dog doo."

"We can't have that." We strolled down the drive, and Anarchy took my hand in his. "This is nice."

A couple walking a dog. It was better than nice.

We took a right at the corner, and Max pulled on his leash.

I pulled back.

Max deigned a glance over his shoulder. He wore a this-is-fun doggy grin on his face and tugged harder.

"Stop that."

"Want me to take him?"

The leash slackened.

"I've got him."

Max lunged, and the leash flew from my hand.

"Darn it, Max." I ran after him—three or four useless steps—then slowed. The dog was faster and wilier than I'd ever be.

He raced around the nearest side yard and into someone's backyard.

"Max!" I stepped onto the lawn.

"Where are you going?"

"To catch him."

"You're trespassing."

I studied the dark house. "I guarantee you, whoever lives here would prefer my trespassing to the damage Max can do to their yard." Thank heavens Pansy, Max's lady love, wasn't with him—she could denude a yard of landscaping faster than the eye could see. "Max," I whisper-yelled. "Get back here."

No surprise, he ignored me.

I slipped through an open wrought-iron gate, rounded the corner to the back lawn, and scanned the darkness.

Pine trees hid the far property line, and a privacy fence obscured the views of the next-door neighbors' yards. A lilac bush sweetened the air, and patio furniture clustered around a kidney-shaped pool.

Max stood at the water's edge.

I rubbed my cheeks, pulling the skin taut.

"Max."

He'd do as he liked. He always did. And right now, he didn't budge.

I squeezed my eyes shut and prayed. When I opened my lids, Max still stood next to the pool, and a body still floated in the water.

"Anarchy," I yelled.

"Can't catch him?" he called.

That was no longer the problem. "I need you."

Perhaps my tone alarmed him because he joined me at a run, stared at the pool for a half-second, then kicked off his shoes and jumped in. The water had to be frigid. Pools without heaters didn't warm to bearable until June's temperatures arrived.

Seconds later, he pulled a woman from the water. I didn't ask if she was dead. Her limp body made the answer obvious. But Anarchy tried mouth-to-mouth. Long minutes passed. He lifted his head and pulled away.

"She's gone."

I gulped.

"Do you know her?"

I edged toward the body, and her face became clear. "I saw her a few hours ago." Why did my lips feel numb?

"Where?"

"Geoffrey Stallard's house." I shivered.

"Who is she?"

"Lilly Frasier."

"Is she married?"

"Yes."

He glanced at the dark house. "Where's her husband?"

Trip Frasier had developed a medical device that he sold for oodles of money. He'd also secured a job with the new owner and attended medical conferences to promote his doohickey. "He travels."

"Can you go next door and call for help?"

"Of course."

I left Max with Anarchy, and my feet flew over the carefully manicured lawn. When I reached the closest house with lights on, I jabbed at the bell.

The front door opened, and Laura Gilchrist gaped at me. "Ellison?"

Relief surged through me. Laura would let me in. "May I please use your telephone?"

She opened the door wide. "Of course. What's wrong?"

I stepped inside and swayed.

"Are you okay?" she demanded.

I hadn't drowned. No one shot me. No one beat me to death with a golf club. But I was not okay. Three bodies in two days will do that to a woman. "I need to call an ambulance."

"An ambulance?" Her eyes widened. "What happened?"

Anarchy had fished her next-door neighbor out of the pool. "Lilly Frasier."

"Lilly?" she squeaked. "Is she alright?"

"We need an ambulance."

"Sit." She pointed me into her living room. "You look as if you might collapse. I'll call, then I'll get you a drink."

I sank onto a blue velvet loveseat, and Laura hurried off to make the call.

I stared at the hands clasped in my lap. How did this keep happening to me? My chest tightened and my jaw ached with unshed tears. Poor Lilly. I didn't find people who died from natural or accidental causes. I'd found countless bodies, each one murdered.

Laura and her husband Charles joined me in the living room. He held out an old-fashioned glass, and Laura spoke, "I called. They're coming."

Charles was a tall man who'd refused to cede an inch to middle-aged spread. His body was fit, but his face was craggy from countless hours spent on golf courses, tennis courts, and pool decks. He'd be handsome were it not for the toupée he insisted on wearing. "Drink this; you'll feel better."

I took the glass and swallowed single-malt scotch. The burn in my throat warmed me. "Thank you."

"What else can we do?" asked Laura.

"Nothing. I should go. Anarchy's with the body." And the dog.

"The body?" Laura pressed her hands to her mouth.

"What happened?" asked Charles.

"Lilly drowned."

Laura squeaked, but Charles sat on the loveseat next to me and patted my knee. "Are you okay?"

"I'm fine." I wasn't.

I WOKE up with an arm wrapped around me and gave a contented sigh.

"What time is it?"

I opened an eye and turned my head toward the clock. "Seven."

Anarchy stiffened. "I overslept. I never oversleep." He sat up. "I'm due at the station at seven thirty."

"Go shower," I told him. "I'll make coffee."

He gave me a quick kiss, swung his legs out of bed, and disappeared into the bathroom.

I hurried downstairs.

Good morning. Mr. Coffee welcomed me with a smile.

I pushed his button. "It is."

You're very happy for a woman who found another body.

"You heard about that?"

You discussed it in the kitchen.

"I'm happy because I'm getting married tomorrow." Tiny needles of guilt pricked at my happiness. I should feel more sadness for Lilly.

Was it murder?

"I don't know. The police found an empty vodka bottle on the kitchen counter."

You have your suspicions—I can tell. What does Anarchy think?

Before I could answer, Grace burst into the kitchen. She offered me a happy grin. "This is your last day as Ellison Russell."

"When it comes to painting, I'll always be Ellison Russell." But she was right. Tomorrow, I'd be Ellison Jones.

"What are you doing today?"

"Errands. Salon. Dress. Staying out of the florist's way."

Her gaze strayed to the Bundt on the counter.

"Don't even think it. I'm taking that cake to Rose Reynolds's sister."

"Then what's for breakfast?"

I finished brewing.

I gave Mr. Coffee a grateful smile, poured myself a cup, and sipped. "Check the fridge."

She opened the door and stared at the contents. "It's all party food. I don't want stuffed mushroom caps for breakfast."

"I can make eggs."

"Very funny." She took out a milk carton. "I'll have cereal."

She shook Super Sugar Crisp into a bowl. "The plan for tonight?"

"Hasn't changed. Family dinner at the club."

She shook her head as if, like me, she anticipated disaster.

Max yawned.

I scowled at him. If he hadn't run off, someone else would have discovered Lilly Frasier's corpse. "You're on my bad side, mister."

"What did he do?"

"He found a body."

"He did not."

"He did."

Max yawned.

"Who? Where?"

"Lilly Frasier."

She tilted her head. "Who?"

"I knew her. Not well. Her kids are older than you." What was wrong with me? Why wasn't grief or horror twisting my stomach into sick knots? Maybe the emotional capacity required to handle more death was too high; I'd reached my limit.

"Was it murder?" Grace asked.

"I don't know."

Anarchy stepped into the kitchen, and I poured coffee and gave him the mug.

Grace frowned at him. "Was it murder?"

Anarchy sipped his coffee. "Lilly Frasier? It looks like an accident."

"What happened?"

I was well past sugarcoating death for Grace. "She drowned in her pool."

I had no concrete reason to believe Lilly's tragic death was murder, but the certainty gnawed at me. "Did you locate Trip?"

"He's in Miami at a medical conference. If it was murder, her husband didn't kill her."

"Unless he hired someone," said Grace.

Grace had grown far too cynical.

"Any marital problems?" Anarchy asked.

"I didn't know her well enough to answer that. I can call Jinx."

"Not my case."

That was a relief. "Is Peters investigating?"

"Rogan."

"I don't know him."

"He's good."

"I'm glad. If she was murdered, she deserves justice."

He lifted a brow.

"I have a gut feeling."

His gaze lingered on my face. "I'll tell Rogan. You're seldom wrong."

Anarchy finished his coffee, gave me a kiss that made me long for our wedding night, and left us.

Grace rolled her eyes at me and put her empty cereal bowl in the sink.

"Dishwasher."

That request earned me a second eyeroll. "You didn't tell Anarchy to put away his mug."

"We're not married yet. Give it a few days."

She snickered. "I'm happy for you, Mom."

The smile inside me wouldn't be denied. I grinned. "Me, too."

Brnng, brnng.

The phone drew our gazes like a horrible car accident on the side of the road.

"Granna?"

"I hope not." I'd rather find another body than talk to Mother about Lilly Frasier.

Brnng, brnng.

"It's too early for her to be up."

Grace shook her head and edged away. "I have school, exams, my whole life ahead of me."

I reached for the receiver. "Hello?"

"Is it true?" Jinx demanded. "Did you find Lilly Frasier's body?"

"News travels fast."

Grace's eyes widened. "Is it Granna?"

I shook my head, and she dragged her hand across her forehead in not-so-mock relief.

"That's a yes?" Jinx demanded.

"Yes," I admitted.

"A busy week, even by your standards."

My lips pursed, but I couldn't argue. Instead, I leaned against the counter. "How well did you know her?"

"We played tennis from time to time."

"Her husband?"

"Smart man. Always thinking technical thoughts. He wasn't much fun."

"Trouble in paradise?"

"No." She sounded mildly surprised. "They were well suited. She drowned?"

"Yes."

"Murder?"

"No idea. Did she drink?"

"A bit." That could mean a cocktail before dinner or cheap gin hidden in the toilet tank. "Why do you ask?"

I had a feeling the police wouldn't appreciate me telling Jinx about the empty vodka bottle the police took into evidence. "Just wondering."

"What aren't you telling me?"

"Give it a rest, Jinx." I stretched the phone's cord and refilled my coffee mug.

"How furious is Frances with your aunt?"

I blinked at the sudden change of subject. "What do you think?"

"I think you may find yet another body this week." She meant Aunt Sis.

"Don't even joke. I'm taking a Bundt to Rose Reynolds's sister today."

"Poor woman. Maybe it's better this way."

"What's better? She was murdered."

"She loved that shop."

"And?"

"There were whispers about asking her to retire."

I'd heard zero whispers. "Why?"

"Profits were down. She wasn't as spry as she once was."

"None of us are."

"The committee members wanted a fresh perspective and updated look."

"It's a thrift shop."

"Don't shoot the messenger."

"Sorry. Which members?"

"Ask Pam Ellis. She's the one who fought to keep Rose."

Grace hefted a backpack onto her shoulder and waved.

"Jinx, Grace is leaving. Can we talk later?"

"Sure thing." She hung up.

I returned the receiver to the cradle. "Good luck on your test, sweetie."

"You too, Mom. Enjoy your last day as a free woman." She grinned and dashed out the door.

I turned to Mr. Coffee.

More coffee?

"Need you ask?"

His answering chuckle was low and dark, but his sunny face clouded. *In Italy, they drink espresso.*

"You know me. I don't drink tiny cups. I need an IV. You'll always hold my heart."

Reassured, Mr. Coffee gave me a saucy wink.

"Good morning." Aggie bustled into the kitchen, her arms filled with grocery bags.

"You've been busy." I took a bag, put it on the counter, and pulled out a wheel of Brie.

"There are no crowds at the market when you go early."

I'd take her word for it.

"I found a body last night." I glanced at Max. "Actually, Max found her."

He wagged his stubby tail.

"Who?"

"Lilly Frasier."

"Murdered?"

I waggled my hand. "Drowned."

"That doesn't answer the question."

"They don't know. A suspicious death?"

"Does Mrs. Walford know?"

"She hasn't called. Yet. But I wanted you to have fair warning."

"Shoo. Get going."

I raised my brows.

"If you leave, when I tell her you can't come to the phone, I won't be lying." She glanced at the Bundt. "Do I need to bake another cake?"

"Trip Frasier is out of town right now. And I'm not disrupting my wedding day to offer condolences. I'll bring him something after the honeymoon."

She nodded.

"By the way, the cake you baked for the Stallards disappeared within five minutes."

She flushed with pleasure. "Go. I'll make a fresh pot while you dress."

Thirty minutes later with a travel mug of coffee in the cupholder and Aggie's Bundt for Rose Reynolds's sister nestled in the car's passenger seat, I returned to the foyer and called, "I'm leaving. I'll be back late this afternoon."

"Don't find any bodies." Aggie's voice carried from the kitchen, where she masterminded culinary delights.

"Very funny."

She stuck her head into the hallway and shook a finger at me. "I'm dead serious."

CHAPTER FIVE

My watch read five minutes till nine. I drove slowly, enjoying the spring flowers and warm sunshine.

The to-do list stretched longer than a fairway—visit the bank, Rose Reynolds's sister's house, and the jeweler for Anarchy's present, make sure my wedding dress fit, and write thank-you notes. I had a full day.

I pulled into the bank's lot, parked the car, and strolled through the door.

Three customers already dotted the lobby—one of whom claimed the manager's attention. Thank heavens. The manager believed a woman's financial talents stretched no further than managing her family household and balancing her checkbook. That Henry's daughter owned the bank and I was the executor (in charge until she reached adulthood) was a heavy cross for him to bear. He overcompensated with a tendency to offer worthless compliments. Lengthy worthless compliments. I simply didn't have the time.

While he was occupied with the customer, I hurried to a teller's window and handed her my deposit.

"Good morning, Mrs. Russell."

I gaped. "You." Out of context, the young woman had looked familiar but foreign. Here, where I was accustomed to seeing her, I immediately recognized her thin face, the sheets of dark hair that framed her cheeks, her narrow chin, and the tentative smile she offered each time I came to her window.

She offered that tremulous smile now. "Is there a problem?"

"You were at the thrift shop on Wednesday."

She flushed. "Yes."

"What were you doing there?"

She lowered her eyes but lifted her chin. "Shopping."

"What did you see?"

Now she frowned. "See?"

"There was a murder."

She clutched the counter, and the color drained from her pretty face.

"What were you doing there?"

"I needed new clothes." She slid my receipt across the counter as if a piece of paper would make me disappear.

"From the thrift shop?"

She nodded.

"Wait here." My pointer finger tapped the counter for emphasis.

This had been my husband's bank. Now it was held in trust for Grace. And I was the trustee. I steeled myself for drivel and entered the manager's office.

He stood immediately. "Mrs. Russell, what a pleasure to see you. What a lovely—" he searched for something to compliment "—necklace."

The gold beads at my neck had belonged to my grandmother, a woman who hadn't suffered fools. She'd have immediately dismissed the man in the blue suit with hair combed over his bald spot as a self-important boob. "Good morning, Mr. Brown." I silently added "nose."

"What brings you to the bank today? How may I help?"

"A telephone, please."

"Use mine." He waved at his phone as if he'd bestowed a great favor.

"Thank you." I picked up the receiver.

He stared at me but didn't leave.

"If you'll excuse me?"

"Oh. Yes. Of course." His cheeks darkened. But he left me alone in his office.

I dialed Anarchy's number.

"Jones."

"I found the woman from the thrift shop."

"Where?"

"I came into the bank to deposit a check. She works here."

"Which branch?"

"The one near the Plaza."

"I'm on my way."

The receiver's click in its cradle meant I had no reason to linger in Mr. Brown's glass-walled office. But I did it anyway. A sigh rose from my toes. When it subsided, I ventured into the lobby, where Mr. Brown, wearing an obsequious smile, sidled up to me.

"What's her name?" I inclined my head toward the teller, who watched me with her lower lip caught in her teeth.

"Cathy Perkins."

"I need to speak with Miss Perkins in your office."

His brows knit. "Problem?"

Not with her work. "She's very pleasant and efficient. A model employee."

"Then why?"

I borrowed a page from Mother's book and lifted a single brow.

He waited for more, but I remained silent.

Flustered, either by my silence or Mother's borrowed

expression, he fetched the young woman, led her to his office, and settled behind his desk.

"Thank you, Mr. Brown, but your presence isn't required."

He colored, but his hands settled over his paunch. As if he were taking my directive under advisement. "I think I should stay."

I swallowed a bitter smile. If Henry had asked to borrow Mr. Brown's office, the bank manager would not have lingered. If Henry had sex on Mr. Brown's desk, the bank manager would have discreetly disappeared into the vault. But I was a woman, so he acted as if he had a right to listen to the conversation. "Oh?"

"If this pertains to Miss Perkins's job performance, I should be here."

"I appreciate your dedication." Could I fire him for annoying me? "But this conversation has nothing to do with Miss Perkins's job."

He didn't budge.

"This is a nice office," I remarked.

He flushed.

"Do you want to keep it?"

He stood and stalked into the lobby.

"About the thrift shop—"

"Am I in trouble? It was my afternoon off." Cathy's worried eyes bored into me. "I work Saturday morning, and Mr. Brown doesn't like to pay overtime, so I got an afternoon." She clasped her hands in her lap. "I wasn't shopping on the bank's time. I promise."

Rather than put a desk between us, I chose the chair next to hers. "You're not in trouble. Not at all."

Her taut shoulders relaxed.

"Do you often shop at the thrift shop?"

"It's what I can afford."

I frowned. "How much do we pay you?"

"I'm not complaining. I like my job." She didn't say she needed her job, but I read it on her worried face.

"How much?" I insisted.

"A dollar-sixty an hour."

I glanced at the lobby where Lester, the head teller, helped a customer. "Lester has four children." I knew because he'd showed me their photographs. I also knew there was no way he could support a family on that wage.

"Lester has been here longer, and..."

"And?"

She stared at her hands folded in her lap. "Mr. Brown says I make a nice second income."

Her bare left hand drew my gaze. "It's not a second income, is it?"

"No, ma'am."

My skin prickled, and my fingers curled. Why was it so hard for men to treat women fairly? I took a deep breath. My argument wasn't with Cathy, it was with...*me*. Oh dear Lord. The buck stopped with me. "In a few minutes, my fiancé will arrive. He'll have questions for you. While you talk with him, I'll chat with Mr. Brown."

"Oh, no." She looked stricken, as if she might cry at any second. "I need this job."

"Trust me, Cathy."

Five minutes later, when Anarchy strode into the lobby, I stepped out of Mr. Brown's office and waved. He walked directly to me, took my hand, and asked, "Everything okay? You look upset."

"There's an unpleasant conversation in my future."

"Oh?"

"I'll be fine. Let me introduce you to Cathy."

He stopped me with a hand on my arm. "Did she see anything?"

"I don't know. We got sidetracked."

Anarchy's brows rose. "You? Sidetracked?"

I nodded. Grimly.

"Do you need me?"

More than I could say. "Not for this. Come meet Cathy."

Anarchy followed me into Mr. Brown's office, took one look at the frightened young woman huddled in the visitor's chair, and donned his most charming smile.

Cathy blinked from its brilliance.

Eschewing the leather chair behind the desk, he sat next to her, rested his elbows on his knees, and leaned toward her. "I'm Detective Jones. Mrs. Russell told me she saw you at the thrift shop earlier this week. Please tell me what happened."

Cathy gave a tiny nod, then shifted her gaze my way.

I offered an encouraging smile, left them in the office, and crossed the lobby to the tellers' windows, where Mr. Brown chatted with Lester. "A moment?"

He turned and forced his face into a polite expression. "Mrs. Russell?"

"I'd like a word." I led him to the empty waiting area, sat in a chair, rested my clasped hands on my knees, and smiled up at him expectantly.

His lips thinned, but he settled into a nearby chair and steepled his fingers.

"It's come to my attention the bank pays women less than men."

He waited for me to elaborate.

My patience with his silence lasted less than three seconds. "Why?"

"What do you mean?" He tilted his head. The question confused him.

"Why pay men and women differently for the same work?"

"Men have families to support."

"And women don't?"

He started an eye roll, then wisely stopped halfway to the ceiling. "There's no need. Besides, it would affect profits."

"I reviewed the initial quarterly reports last week. The bank can easily afford equal pay."

"There's no point in investing in a young woman's career."

I raised my brows.

"Women get married, get pregnant, and leave. Then we have to train someone new."

"Equal pay for equal work, Mr. Brown. It's the bank's new policy."

He shot a venomous look at his office, where Anarchy spoke with Cathy.

"When I return from my honeymoon, I expect to find Miss Perkins at her job, being paid the same hourly rate as the male tellers." No employee of mine would be paid so poorly that her only option for new clothes was a thrift shop.

He offered me a superior smile. "I don't think you've considered the ramifications. This policy won't just affect Miss Perkins. Thirty percent of the bank's employees are women."

"Then thirty percent are due a pay raise."

"The board—"

"Answers to me. If this is something you cannot do, please tell me, and I'll find someone who can." I stared straight into his pale blue eyes. "Miss Perkins's work environment will remain pleasant. Do we understand each other?"

The man looked like he'd sucked on a lemon, but he nodded.

I stood. "A pleasure chatting with you, Mr. Brown." With the pay issue settled, I couldn't wait to hear what Cathy Perkins had told Anarchy. But I could hardly go charging into Mr. Brown's office.

Instead, I stepped outside, where the morning sun warmed my shoulders. After a few minutes, Anarchy joined me. The expression in his eyes warmed me from the inside out.

"What did Cathy say?" I asked.

"She bought a navy-blue skirt, paid cash, and left."

"Did she see anyone else in the shop?"

"She saw you and Avery Stallard. Mrs. Stallard entered from the back of the shop and demanded Rose's assistance. Immediately."

"And?"

"Rose finished ringing up Cathy's purchase and walked Cathy to the front door. As Cathy was leaving, she heard a bell."

"There's a doorbell at the back door for donation drop-offs. The door's kept locked."

Anarchy frowned. "You walked in with your boxes."

I thought back. "The door was ajar when I arrived."

"Is that usual?"

"No. Totally against the rules. But when someone's brought multiple boxes, they'll stick in a doorjamb." Also, the women who used that door were volunteers or donors. Rose could make all the rules she wanted. Didn't mean they'd be followed, not when there were no consequences for breaking them.

"Did the door close when you left?"

"I honestly don't remember. I wasn't surprised to find it open."

"So Rose opened the door for Avery and let her carry in her donation. She didn't help?"

"Never. Especially not when there was a customer in the store."

"Presumably Avery closed the door when she finished bringing in boxes."

"Because Cathy heard the bell ring?"

Anarchy nodded and tucked a strand of hair behind my ear. "Rose walked Cathy to the front exit and locked the door behind her."

"That young woman is so lucky."

Anarchy's brows rose.

"She was in the shop with the killer."

"The shop closes at five. Why did Rose lock the front door early?"

"That's easy. Shoplifting can be a problem. If Rose had to go to the back, she'd lock the front door before she went."

"According to Cathy, the bell rang at a quarter till five."

"And I arrived at five." Fifteen minutes for two murders. That was chilling. I shivered in the sunshine.

Anarchy glanced at the cloudless blue sky and frowned. "Are you headed home?"

"I have a Bundt cake for Rose's sister and a million errands. Also, the florist says I interfere. He doesn't want me around."

A thoroughly provoking quirk curled Anarchy's lips.

"What time do your parents arrive?"

His smile faded. "Shortly after one."

"Are you picking them up?"

"They prefer to catch a cab."

The people-pleasing, good-girl, you're-marrying-their-son part of me nudged—*offer to fetch them*. The sane part of me kept that bit of insanity quiet.

"I can go to Rose's sister's house with you," Anarchy offered.

"You could," I agreed.

"But?"

"She might tell me things she'd never tell a cop."

"Rose wasn't the target."

"Maybe Rose gossiped about the League members. Maybe she was worried about someone hanging around the shop. Maybe—"

Anarchy cut me off with a quick kiss. "Maybe you should have been a detective."

If anyone saw me kiss him back, Mother would hear of it and I'd get a lecture about inappropriate public displays of affection. I kissed him anyway.

"Be careful." He kissed the tip of my nose.

"I always am."

"I won't bother arguing that. I'll see you tonight." He opened the car's driver's side door for me. "Call if you need me."

"Promise." I slipped behind the wheel and slid the key in the ignition.

"This time next week, we'll be in Italy."

"You'll be exhausted from looking at little churches with unbelievable frescoes."

His eyes sparkled. "Can't wait. Talk to you soon."

Reluctantly, I put the car in gear and drove south and east.

Kansas City's planners had created a city on a grid. Street numbers began at the river and grew higher as they went south. The city's east and west sides were divided by Main Street. For a city its size, there were very few winding roads. And unlike their neighbors on the Kansas side, the city planners didn't take a name like Wenonga and make it a place, a circle, a road, a lane, and a terrace.

Rose Reynolds's sister, Maggie Hatch, lived well south of my usual stomping grounds. But thanks to the grid, I found her house without any trouble and parked at the curb amongst a collection of Buicks, Fords, and Chevrolets. The cars might be different from the ones that lined the street in front of the Stallard home, but the sentiment was the same. Friends had gathered to offer Maggie their love and support.

My low-heeled pumps tapped against the concrete walk. Maggie's house was small, with tan siding and a well-maintained yard. Begonias in terracotta pots bloomed on her front steps, and yews formed an even hedge beneath the front windows.

I rang the bell and a middle-aged woman answered the door.

"Good morning." I held out the cake. "I brought this for Maggie Hatch."

The woman stood aside. "Maggie's in the living room."

I took a left and entered a tiny living room that held a worn recliner, a floral couch, a coffee table, ten million family photos, a television, at least ten women clutching handkerchiefs, and the smell of stale cigarettes. A woman who looked like Rose sat on one end of the couch. She regarded me with watery eyes. "Are you from the Junior League?"

They hadn't sent me. "Not as an official representative, but that's how I knew Rose." I held up the cake, and the woman who'd opened the door took it from my hands.

Maggie gave a curt nod, as if I'd passed a test. "So many nice women have stopped by. Rosie was well-liked."

"She was," I agreed.

"Sit, please."

My choices were the recliner or the floral couch. I picked the couch.

"May I offer you coffee?"

"Please."

"Ann?" Maggie's damp eyes searched for the woman who'd let me in. "Would you please fetch a cup of coffee for..."

"Ellison," I supplied. "Ellison Russell."

Maggie's eyes widened. "You're the one who found her."

"I'm so sorry for your loss."

Her chin trembled, and she pressed her fingers to her mouth. "Rosie loved that place."

"Anyone could tell."

Maggie stared over my shoulder as if she saw something other than the living room. The past? "They wanted her to retire." A bitter ribbon laced through her words.

"Oh?"

Maggie's lips pinched. "She couldn't afford to retire."

Friends who worked retail had shared that the job didn't pay well. They worked twenty hours a week for the employee discount. Their husbands claimed they worked on the barter system. If stores on the Plaza didn't pay well, a thrift shop on the edge of the city east side certainly couldn't.

"There was talk about forcing her."

"Forcing her?"

"To retire."

Who'd told me that? I pushed the question away and focused on Maggie. "Rose was respected. And well-liked. The League would never have forced her retirement."

Maggie gave me a you're-too-stupid-to-live look. "How long have you been a League member?"

"Nearly twenty years."

"Active or sustainer?"

The League didn't allow members to go sustaining, which excused them from active requirements, until they hit forty. With that birthday fast approaching, I was counting the days until I hung up my volunteer apron for good. "Active. For now."

"The League looks out for the League."

Maggie made it sound like a criminal enterprise and not an organization of women dedicated to volunteerism in their community. Granted, those volunteers worked their fingers to the bone to help people they'd never allow as members. But the volunteerism counted for something.

"You truly believe the League would have made Rose retire?"

"Rose believed it."

I laced my fingers. "She must have felt betrayed."

Maggie snorted, then regarded me closely. "And now she's dead."

Was she suggesting the League had killed Rose because she refused to retire? I'd heard crazy theories before—lots of them—but none crazier than that.

Ann placed a mug of coffee on the table next to me, and I murmured, "Thank you."

"Aunt Rose asked those women if she could stay until she turned seventy. That's when her annuities started paying. They—" she grimaced and took a breath "—they told her no."

What could I say?

"She put up with hoity-toity attitudes, volunteers who didn't show, donors who filled boxes with moth-eaten sweaters and holey jeans, and customers who stole. For decades. And what did it get her?"

I didn't dare answer.

"To be punched in the teeth as she neared the finish line."

"Ann," said Maggie. "It's not Mrs. Russell's fault."

Ann stared out the front window for long seconds. "I apologize, but Aunt Rosie deserved better, and we all knew it." She pressed a fist against her mouth and squeezed her eyes shut. "That damned store. She gave it everything, and it got her killed."

CHAPTER SIX

The Plaza in springtime was spectacular. Colorful banners shared light pole arms with enormous pots of pink petunias. Begonias and geraniums and bright yellow marigolds filled flower beds. Women on the sidewalk smiled at the sun in their faces. I needed bright and happy and hopeful after my visit with Rose's family.

I set aside the League as an evil enterprise, found a spot on the street, parked, and dashed into the jewelry store, where the carpets were lush, the air smelled of luxury, and the lighting was endlessly flattering.

The store's charismatic owner kissed my cheek. "Ellison, I thought we might see you today."

"Is it ready?"

"Give me a minute." He disappeared into an office, but quickly returned with a box.

I opened the lid.

"It's as you asked. The date engraved on the top line then, 'From this day till the end of time' below."

My eyes misted. "It's perfect."

"Shall we wrap it for you?"

"Please."

I admired diamond stud earrings while a clerk expertly wrapped Anarchy's watch.

"Should we bill you?"

I blinked at the total. "I'll write a check."

The owner presented me with a handsome shopping tote, and I waited until I was on the sidewalk to stash it in the depths of my shoulder bag. Mother once warned me that thieves targeted women carrying bags from jewelry stores. Of all the advice she ever gave me, not walking down a sidewalk advertising a recent purchase from a jewelry store was what stuck.

My watch, not nearly as nice as the one I'd purchased for Anarchy, read half past ten.

Coffee and a mid-morning pastry called to me, and I strolled to the French bakery, stopping to window shop on my way. A Kelly green wrap dress with navy piping at Harzfeld's caught my eye, but I resisted. Soon I'd be shopping in Italy. I'd just spent a small fortune. Three Kelly green dresses already hung in my closet. Feeling virtuous, I walked on by.

When I arrived at La Bonne Bouchée, the hostess led me to a small table, and I ordered a café au lait and palmier. While I waited for the coffee, I took a small box of note cards from my bag, considered the top card, and traced the monogram with my fingertip. EWR was wrong—or would be in a day. I added a trip to Bennett Schneider for new stationery to the tasks I needed to accomplish, pulled the list of gifts from my handbag, and began.

The first line was the easiest.

Dear Sydney,

Just a quick note to thank you for the gorgeous negligee. It will be joining me on an Italian honeymoon.

Truth? I'd never be able to wear the near see-through gown without blushing.

I'm so grateful we were able to spend some time together during this special week. I treasure your friendship and thank you sincerely for your thoughtful gift.

Fond regards,

Ellison

One note down, forty-seven to go.

I addressed the envelope, licked a stamp, and started on the next note.

The garter belt Judy Grant gave me was suitable for a porn star. I nibbled the end of the pen and pondered how to thank her. That particular note could wait until I hit a groove.

"Your coffee, ma'am."

I looked up from the blank note card and smiled at the waiter. "Thank you."

"Ellison?" Dot waved at me from the pastry counter.

I waved back, and she walked to my table.

"May I join you while they prepare my order?"

I inclined my head toward the empty chair. "Please."

"Coffee, ma'am?" the waiter asked.

"No, I can't stay." Dot sat and watched the waiter walk away. Then she leaned halfway over the table and whispered, "Can you talk to your fiancé? They're checking our alibis."

Anarchy had mentioned the Stallards didn't have alibis. I maintained a neutral expression. "I'm sorry, Dot. Getting mixed up in a homicide investigation is awful."

"No one in my family killed Avery."

"Then the police won't find anything. They have to ask questions, Dot. If only to clear you."

"Tori and I were shopping," she insisted. Her arms crossed over her chest. "Together."

"If you told Detective Peters, he'll check it out."

"We went to a mall. No place where we knew salesclerks." Dot's gaze shifted to the pedestrians on the sidewalk outside.

A sudden certainty that she was lying took hold of me. "Did you buy anything?"

"No."

"That's too bad. A receipt would prove you were there. Does the mall have security cameras?"

"Can't you explain to your fiancé that we're innocent?" Dot's voice was so loud it attracted attention from the other tables. She ducked her head and scowled.

"Murder investigations don't work that way." My word wasn't good enough. Not for Anarchy. Definitely not for Peters. Their investigation would expose secrets. And those secrets might have nothing to do with Avery and Rose's deaths. Was that what had Dot so worried? "Dot, we've been friends since preschool. You can talk to me. What's bothering you?"

For a brief second, her expression softened.

My fingers crossed in my lap. *Please don't let me be wrong. Please don't let her confess.*

The softness on Dot's face dissipated into the coffee-and-sugar-scented air, and a hard-edged cynicism took its place. "You'll repeat whatever I say."

I didn't dispute her claim.

"Promise me you won't go to the police, and I'll tell you."

I couldn't make that promise. "Don't tell me."

She stood. Abruptly. "I shouldn't have bothered you."

I reached for her hand. "It's no bother. I'll talk to Anarchy. I think you're innocent, but the police will still investigate. They absolutely refuse to take my word for these things."

She jerked her hand free. "This isn't a joke."

Her words stung like a slap on the cheek. "I found two dead women. I'm well aware."

She stepped backward. "Talking to you was a mistake. I'm sorry I disturbed your coffee." She turned on her heel, collected her bag of pastries from the counter, and left.

Dot was deeply worried about Avery's murder. Did she suspect one of her siblings? Her father?

Half my coffee disappeared before I could bring myself to start another note.

Dear Eloise,

A quick note to thank you for the gorgeous satin teddy. It's already in my suitcase packed for Italy.

Thank you also for sharing part of our celebration. It meant the world to have you with me.

Fond regards,

Ellison

I returned to Judy Grant's name on the list and tapped my pen on the table's edge. Why a garter belt? And how could I write a thank you note for it? I stared out the window and thought. Not a single idea came to me, but I did spot Pam Ellis on the sidewalk. I caught her eye and beckoned her inside.

A moment later, she stood next to my table.

"Can you join me?" I asked.

"For a moment. I'm due at a fitting."

"Coffee?"

"No. Nothing, thank you." She sat in the empty chair and gave me an expectant smile.

"I visited Maggie Hatch today."

"Oh?" Her smile disappeared, and her voice flattened.

"She shared with me the League's plans to replace Rose."

Pam winced, and her shoulders sagged. "I was trying to stop that. Rose gave the League decades of service. The least we could do was let her retire on her schedule, not ours."

That sounded like Pam. Kind and fair.

"What was the problem?"

"Some of the younger girls wanted a fresh perspective."

"Rose knew?"

"She did." Pam fixed her gaze on her lap. "Running a thrift shop isn't a high-paying job. That said, we should have paid her more and provided a better retirement plan." She rested her hands on the table and laced her fingers. "The poor woman was facing an old age spent flirting with poverty."

"Her sister mentioned something about annuities."

Pam stared at my coffee cup as if she were second guessing her decision not to order one of her own. "Two years. That's all she was asking. But Gwen Lewis and her coven wouldn't stand for it."

"Who told Rose?"

Pam flushed, and I had my answer.

"She deserved time to plan, time to find another job."

Neither of us stated the obvious—that a woman in her late sixties, who'd spent decades managing a thrift shop exactly as she saw fit while barking at volunteers and customers alike, would have difficulty landing employment.

"She was hurt. And angry. She felt betrayed and resentful," said Pam. "And I didn't blame her."

"What was her plan?"

"I don't know," Pam replied. "But I'm sure she had one. Her biggest fear was becoming a burden to her sister and niece."

"The situation reflects poorly on the League. Rose might have gone to the press."

"Gwen—" Pam's tone twisted the name into "evil crone" "—believed Rose had too much loyalty to expose us." Again, Pam's gaze fixed on my coffee cup. "If Rose didn't make a stink, I would have." Her lips thinned, and she cleared her throat. "It doesn't matter now."

I'd never considered how the League treated its paid employees. "What about the other women on the League's payroll? Are they fairly compensated?"

"We should look into that."

We? It was one thing to walk into the bank and demand equal pay for women. I could act unilaterally. To join a compensation committee at the League meant endless meetings and circular discussions that might melt my brain. "Pam, I don't have room on my plate."

She frowned. Deeply. Her obvious disappointment wounded me. A flesh wound—not near severe enough to compel me to sign up for hell.

"I'll consider it." How had *that* escaped my lips?

Pam nodded. "Thank you." She glanced at her watch and stood. "The League is planning a memorial presentation at the thrift shop."

"You're kidding."

"I am not."

"That's a terrible idea." Seeing as her family blamed the League and the thrift shop for Rose's death, I doubted they'd be amenable. "Has anyone talked to Rose's family about this?"

"The presentation was Gwen's idea." A wicked smile touched Pam's lips. "Rose knew who was behind her forced retirement. I imagine her family does too." Maggie Hatch would give Gwen hell. In public.

There was a reason I admired Pam Ellis. Kind. Fair. And slightly devious.

She left me, and I finished my coffee and nibbled at the palmier. Jitters made eating impossible, so I abandoned the pastry, paid the bill, and strolled to Bennett Schneider.

"Is two weeks too long for delivery?" asked Lois, the woman who'd assisted me in selecting new stationery—fold-over notes and cards made from creamy, heavy stock—with my new monogram in a cerulean blue.

"Two weeks is fine." I wouldn't need stationery until Anarchy and I returned from Italy. "May I please use your phone?"

"Of course."

"Do you have a phone book?"

"May I look up a number for you?"

"The Alameda."

Lois squinted and searched for the number, and I peeked into my handbag at Anarchy's wrapped watch. Would he like it? Was it too extravagant?

"There you are." Lois slipped a phone number written on note paper topped with Bennett Schneider's signature seal in front of me. "You can use Bob's office."

"Thank you." I settled behind Bob's desk, called the Alameda, and asked for Karma's room.

"Hello."

"It's me."

"Ellison." Her voice was warm. "How's your last full day as a single woman?"

"Busy. I'm on the Plaza, on my way to Swanson's to try on my dress. Would you like to meet me there? Or we could meet for lunch at Nabil's at one."

"I'd love to see your dress. I'll meet you at Swanson's."

"Second floor. Couture."

"I'll head over this minute."

We hung up, and I rose from Bob's chair and returned to the shop. "Many thanks, Lois."

"Thank you for coming in, Mrs. Russell."

I stepped into the sunshine and headed toward Swanson's.

"Ellison?"

I turned. Jane Addison stood a few feet behind me.

"Are you okay? I heard about last night."

I'd barred Lilly Frasier from my mind. But with six words the horror rushed toward me, washed over me, and left me paddling in a bottomless pool of guilt. "Such a terrible tragedy."

"What an awful shock." Her gaze searched my face. "Has your fiancé discovered who killed Avery Stallard?"

"And Rose." Everyone forgot about poor Rose.

"Right. And Rose."

"If he has, he hasn't told me. Detective Peters is actually the lead detective."

"That's right. You're leaving on your honeymoon."

"Exactly."

She nodded, as if Anarchy's letting Peters investigate was an act of genius. "It's probably better this way."

"Better?"

She flushed. "It might be uncomfortable for you if your new husband arrested one of the Stallards."

"You think one of them is guilty?"

She held up her hands. "I didn't say that."

I raised a brow.

"They all have motives. Angry motives."

"Just because someone has a reason to commit murder doesn't mean they act."

"They have to be suspects."

I didn't respond.

"Oh, come on, Ellison. Everyone in town knows the police are looking at them. I heard all about Sydney's revelation at your luncheon."

Too good a story not to share. I'd shared it with Anarchy. Of course Jane had heard it.

"So? Who's the top suspect?"

"Jane, I've been so busy with the wedding, I haven't paid the slightest attention to the case." Not entirely true, but close.

She lowered a brow and tilted her disbelieving head.

"Perhaps Rose was the target," I suggested.

"You can't be serious."

"Why not?"

"Who'd want to kill Rose Reynolds?"

"Hundreds of women." Arriving late for a shift could land a woman in real trouble. And not showing up? Unable to find a substitute, Daisy once drove back from a resort in the Ozarks to meet her volunteer requirement.

"No one killed Rose over volunteer hours."

"You sound so sure," I murmured.

"Rose enjoyed her power. Probably too much. But no one commits murder because they're short thirty minutes of volunteer time."

Contrariness took over. "Rose might have had hidden depths," I suggested. "Secrets."

"Then why was Avery beaten?"

Instead of ceding Jane's excellent point, I gave a brief nod. "Jane, I could speculate with you all afternoon, but I need to pick up my wedding dress."

"I won't keep you." She kissed the air next to my cheek. "You will be a radiant bride and I wish you every happiness."

"Thank you."

"Let's meet for lunch or cocktails when you return from Italy."

"I'd love that."

"Talk soon." She waggled her fingers and ducked into Halls.

I put murders and drownings out of my head and continued to the end of the block. Of all the marvelous stores on the Plaza, Swanson's was my favorite. I rode the escalator to the second floor and Esme, who always helped me, stepped forward.

"Is it ready?" I asked.

Esme grinned. "Ready to try it on?"

"I am." My Aunt Sis married Gordon in a fabulous suit. She'd inspired me to eschew a traditional wedding dress. Instead, I'd selected a Halston A-line gown. The color was white, but every inch of the dress was covered with crystal beads that caught the light and reflected a gentle rainbow.

Esme led me to the largest dressing room and helped me into the scoop-neck dress.

"You look beautiful, Mrs. Russell." She laughed softly. "It may take me a while to get used to Mrs. Jones."

"Me, too."

"You'll make a beautiful bride. I'm very happy for you."

Someone tapped on the dressing room door. "Ellison? It's Karma."

"It's my sister," I explained.

Esme opened the door, and Karma spotted me on the carpeted riser surrounded by mirrors. "Wow. You're absolutely gorgeous. If Anarchy weren't already hopelessly in love with you, that dress would push him over the edge."

Why was I suddenly misty?

"Has Frances seen it?"

That dried the unexpected wetness in my eyes. "She's the one who insisted on an evening wedding." I'd wanted to exchange vows earlier in the day. Noon. Followed by a luncheon. But Mother prevailed. Then we'd argued about the time—seven thirty (black-tie optional) or eight (black tie)—till our fingers curled in anticipation of throttling each other. I'd put my foot down. Seven thirty.

"Mother might voice her opinion." *You're wearing that?* already rang in my ears. "But she'll get over it." Eventually.

I turned to Esme. "Karma and I are grabbing a bite to eat next door." My fingers caressed the delicate beads. "May I pick this up when we've finished?"

"Now that we know it's perfect, we'll deliver it. We can have it there by four."

The dress wouldn't be jammed in my car? "I'd be grateful. Thank you."

Esme and Karma stepped outside, and I changed my clothes. When I emerged from the dressing room, Karma tore her gaze from a display of silk scarves. "Are you ready?" she asked. "I'm famished."

Lunch had seemed like a good idea, but I wasn't sure I could eat a bite.

Three minutes later, Karma and I smiled at each other over a table at Nabil's as the waiter left us to fetch the bottle of Champagne Karma had ordered.

I ignored the menu. "I have a question."

"Shoot."

"Are you paid the same as your male colleagues?"

Karma blinked as if I'd surprised her.

"I ask because I stopped by the bank this morning and discovered an imbalance."

"I work on commission." Karma was a stock broker. "So I'm paid the same. But I'm an exception."

"I also discovered that the League, an organization run by women, didn't pay Rose Reynolds enough to save for retirement."

"Are you sure?"

"What do you mean?"

"Maybe she didn't save."

I hadn't considered that.

The waiter appeared, opened the Champagne, and poured golden bubbles into two flutes.

Karma lifted her glass. "To happiness."

Anarchy and I had happiness covered. "To a wedding day without drama."

Karma grinned. "Why don't you wish for something easier? World peace? An end to hunger? The ERA passing?"

She was right. Tomorrow would be a rollercoaster. But I didn't care as long as when it ended, I was Mrs. Anarchy Jones.

CHAPTER SEVEN

Karma ate chicken in a lemon caper sauce as I picked at a salad. "Too nervous to eat?" she asked.

I pushed a radicchio leaf around my plate and breathed deep. Without the distraction of shopping or wondering how to thank Judy Grant for the X-rated garter belt, my thoughts had turned to Lilly. "I found another body."

Karma choked on a caper. "You're kidding."

"Nope."

"When?"

"Last night."

"Murder?"

"She drowned."

"Doesn't answer my question."

"I don't have a definitive answer."

Karma offered a sympathetic wince. "What happened?"

I told her about the moonlit walk with Anarchy, Max's stubborn dash into the backyard, and Lilly Frasier's body floating in the pool.

Her forehead puckered. "Did you know her well?"

Lilly and I had been nodding acquaintances. My circle included women with whom I'd grown up, women with whom I did committee work, women who had children around Grace's age, and women whose husbands belonged to the same club as I did (I held a widow's membership). Lilly fell into none of those buckets. And even if we'd brushed elbows every day, we wouldn't have become friends. "Not well."

"Was her death related to the murders?"

I froze with a bite of salad halfway to my mouth. I hadn't considered that, but with my luck, Karma's question was on target. A third body was too coincidental. "That would mean someone has killed three different ways."

"A gun, a brutal assault, a drowning." Karma ticked grisly deaths on her fingers.

I didn't need the reminder.

Karma lifted her water goblet to her lips. "I've been thinking..."

"Yes?"

"What happened at the thrift shop? Who died first? Why didn't the other woman run?"

"The killer entered through the shop's back door and grabbed the nearest weapon." I frowned at my salad as if it were responsible for what came next. "Henry's seven iron."

"But the killer had a gun. Why did he need a golf club?"

"Anarchy says the killer wanted Avery to suffer."

"Rose was at the wrong place at the wrong time?"

"If the killer followed Avery to the store, he or she had to know there would be at least one employee."

"So the manager was collateral damage and got a merciful death?"

I put down my fork. My appetite had completely disappeared.

Karma tapped her chin. "What if you hadn't donated a golf club?"

"The shop has baseball bats and hockey sticks galore."

"Would the killer know that?"

"Don't most thrift shops have used sporting equipment?" The only thrift shop I'd ever entered was the League's, and it carried used ice skates, secondhand tennis rackets, baseball and ice hockey equipment, golf clubs, old skis, and badminton and croquet sets.

Karma ceded my point with a brief nod. "So how did it happen? The killer walks into the shop—"

"Through the back door. He entered through the stock room. The bell rang, and either Avery or Rose let him in."

"They knew him?"

"Everyone seems to think so."

"Okay." Karma rubbed her chin. "She lets him in. Why didn't you find her body in the stock room?"

"Maybe the killer worried there were customers out front. He wanted to make sure there weren't ten witnesses in the shop."

"Fair enough. So the killer grabs Henry's club, follows Avery into the shop, sees Rose and shoots her, then beats Avery to death?"

"That sounds so calculating." We'd assumed a crime of passion. I closed my eyes and pictured a shadowy hand pulling a trigger, saw Rose fall backward, felt Avery's terror. "Maybe Avery tried to run."

Karma paled. "So he beat her?"

"Rose is dead. With her out of the way, the killer whacks Avery with a golf club until she's dead."

"Okay. What about the drowned woman?"

"I have no idea." I studied my lap as if the linen napkin draped across my legs held the answer. "She knew something about the murders? That, or I'm wrong, and she just drowned."

"Do you believe that?"

I looked up. "Given my track record? Chances are good she was murdered."

"Will Anarchy let this go and focus on the wedding and your honeymoon? A trip to Italy with a husband who's contemplating murder doesn't sound terribly romantic."

Anarchy solved cases. He worried at them till the killer became clear. Even if he wasn't the lead investigator, this was one case I didn't want to take on my honeymoon. I forced a smile. "It doesn't seem possible we're getting married tomorrow." A year ago I'd been unhappily married with the prospect of divorce (tied to Grace's high-school graduation) still years away. I ignored Henry's infidelities. I gritted my teeth and complied when Mother issued directives. I painted within my comfort zone. So much had changed. The muscles in my face loosened till the smile was genuine. "I'm incredibly lucky."

"I don't know how you do it."

"Do what?"

"Stay so positive. If it were me, I'd be huddled in a corner with my arms wrapped around my knees and my eyes screwed shut."

If anyone but Karma (or Libba) said that, I'd hear implied judgment. *Ellison, you're unfeeling. Ellison, how can you smile and think about your wedding when three women are dead?* Or maybe those comments came from my inner critic, who had no trouble producing acidic dialogue (she took after Mother).

The champagne bubbles popped at the top of my glass as I searched for a reply. "I don't mean to be cold or unfeeling."

"That's not what I meant. Please don't take it that way. You're neither cold nor unfeeling."

"I found three dead women this week, and rather than grieve, I'm focused on my wedding."

"They weren't close friends. They weren't family. You can't stop living because someone dies." She frowned. "You know that."

"I do." Take *that*, inner critic. "But sometimes it's nice to be reminded."

"You deserve a perfect wedding, a perfect honeymoon, and an epic happily ever after." She patted her mouth with her napkin. "Get married. Go to Italy. And if you find bodies in Venice, pretend blindness."

I lifted my glass. "I'll drink to that."

We clinked our glasses.

"Enough about me." This talk of murder and dead bodies was too dark. "What's happening in your life?"

"Dad wants me to move."

"Where?"

"Here." Her gaze was hopeful. "Would you mind?"

"Mind?" A grin split my face. "I'd love it!"

"And Frances?"

"If it makes Daddy happy, Mother adapts."

"That's not exactly healthy."

"That's Mother. For women of her era, men come first. Always." That was the bargain. Daddy made the money, and Mother stayed home, raised children, and built him a pleasant life. Mother and Daddy were too set in their ways to change now. "Are you serious about this?"

"Mom moved to Portland. There's no one keeping me in San Francisco. And I can get a job anywhere."

"Then do it. Move to Kansas City."

"I have to sell my house in California. Find a place to live."

"You can stay with me—with us—while you look. I'll introduce you to Jane Addison. She'll find you the perfect place."

"I'm not staying with newlyweds. I'll rent."

"You're serious about this?"

"You really wouldn't mind?"

"I'll mind if you don't move." I rubbed my palms together. "This is the best news ever."

"And Marjorie?"

"Marjorie lives in Ohio and always will." The sister with whom I grew up was less enamored with the sister we discovered than I was.

"This won't upset your relationship?"

It would. Marjorie would be jealous and competitive and petty. "Marjorie will fuss, then she'll settle down. When is this happening?"

"I'll put my house on the market when I get home."

I reached across the table and took her hand. "This is such wonderful news. I will love having you here."

Karma's eyes widened, and I glanced over my shoulder. Hunter Tafft, the man Mother hoped I'd marry, stood behind my chair.

Had they been introduced? I couldn't remember. I stood, accepted a kiss on the cheek, and gave Hunter a quick hug. "Hunter, have you met my sister, Karma?"

Hunter didn't react to my having a new sister. Karma's existence had been big news a few months ago. That Harrington Walford had fathered a love child still stiffened Mother's spine, even if Karma had been conceived before Mother and Daddy fell in love. "A pleasure."

"Karma is moving to Kansas City."

"Welcome. I didn't mean to interrupt your lunch, but I wanted to offer Ellison my best wishes."

"Thank you, Hunter."

He kissed my cheek, nodded to Karma, and left us.

"Handsome man." Karma's gaze followed Hunter back to his table.

"Single." I resumed my seat.

"Oh?" Her voice was deceptively mild.

"Divorced three times." Hunter carried hefty baggage.

A wrinkle creased her forehead. "Oh."

"Mother's convinced Hunter hasn't met the right woman."

"And you?"

"He's a good friend. I think Mother may be right."

"Three times?"

Karma and Hunter together? It was a fabulous idea. "When you move here—"

She held up a hand. "Romance is not my friend."

"A year ago, I'd have said the same." Anarchy had changed so much in my life. My eyes misted as my gaze sought the ring sparkling on my left hand. "How are you spending the rest of the afternoon?"

"No plans."

"I'm having my nails done. Care to join me?"

Karma glanced at her unvarnished fingertips.

"I'd love to, but don't I need an appointment?"

I waved that away. "They'll fit you in. I promise."

After lunch, we strolled to Salon Kunz, where the receptionist welcomed me with a smile. "Good afternoon, Mrs. Russell."

"Good afternoon, Lynn. This is my sister Karma. Would you please fit her in for nails with me?"

Lynn's forehead puckered, and she studied her book. A few seconds passed, then her wrinkles cleared. "Certainly." She sounded triumphant.

"You're the best."

Becky, my manicurist, joined us at the reception desk. "Good afternoon, Mrs. Russell."

Karma and I followed her into the Kunz's black and chrome salon and sat at adjoining stations.

I'd brought a bottle of Dior's Polaris Pink that I pulled from my handbag and gave to Becky.

She accepted the bottle and eyed the color. "Pretty. Do you want to take off your ring?"

I slipped off Anarchy's diamond and tucked it into the zippered compartment in my handbag.

"Marla will be here in just a moment," Becky said to Karma. "Would you like to pick a color?"

Karma nodded and went to the display, where pink, red, and peach hues awaited her consideration.

Becky soaked a cotton ball in acetone, removed my existing polish, and put my left hand in a glass bowl filled with lavender-scented water. "I heard you found Mrs. Stallard's body."

I stiffened, then forced myself to relax. Becky gossiped like other people breathed. I'd have quit her long ago, but she never, ever mentioned clients and she did a lovely job on my nails. "I did."

She eyed my right hand. "Are we shortening?"

"Please."

Becky nodded and soaked a fresh cotton ball. "She was a client."

"Oh?"

"Red. Oval." She frowned. Becky had talked me into squared nails by telling me ovals were too 1960s. "Wednesday mornings at ten."

Interesting. "Did she come this Wednesday?"

Becky nodded.

That meant Avery had sat in this chair hours before her murder. "How did she seem?"

"The same." Becky glanced at the empty station next to us and whispered, "Mrs. Stallard didn't like her husband's children."

I amended my assessment of Becky's gossip—she didn't talk about living clients. "Why not?"

"She said they looked down on her."

"Did she give specific examples?"

"She said Tori mocked her taste. They didn't invite her to their children's birthday parties. They tried to turn their father against her." She glanced at Marla's empty station. "She also said one of them had tried to get around her, but she'd turned the tables and got the best of them."

Dread settled in my stomach. "Which one?"

Becky shrugged, pulled clippers from a jar, and cut the tip off my thumbnail. "This length or shorter?"

I glanced at the nail. "Shorter."

Marla slipped behind her station. "Good afternoon, Mrs. Russell."

Karma took her seat, and Marla claimed her left hand.

I stared at Marla's tidy station. "Becky was just telling me Avery Stallard was here on Wednesday."

Marla nodded. "So awful. Becky and I each lost clients this week."

"Oh?"

"Avery Stallard and Lilly Frasier." Marla gazed at Karma's fingers as if they were fascinating. "I heard you found both of them."

"I did."

Marla looked up sharply, and Becky, who'd been gently pushing at my cuticles, shoved hard enough to hurt. I jerked my hand, and Becky murmured an apology.

"It was an accident?" asked Marla.

"As far as I know." I stared at the woman across from me. "Why do you ask? Do you think someone killed Lilly?"

The two manicurists exchanged a loaded glance.

Then Marla shifted her gaze to Karma's cuticles. "Last time Mrs. Frasier came in, she swanned around like she'd just been elected president of the Junior League."

Lilly being elected to anything was less likely than Mother growing her hair to her waist and trading her Chanel for hemp tunics.

"When was this?"

"Yesterday morning."

Apparently getting one's nails done put one on the fast track for death. "Oh?"

Becky and Marla traded a second look, then Becky asked, "Have you seen *Shampoo*? I keep meaning to go."

We talked of movies. Wondered if Burt Reynolds and Dinah Shore would get back together. Then debated who was sexier – Burt or Warren? I chose Steve McQueen, but only because he looked like Anarchy (Anarchy had much better eyes).

When our nails dried, Karma stood and hugged me. "I'll see you tonight."

"Do you need a ride to the club?"

"Sis and Gordon are taking me." To appease Mother, we'd chosen the club as the site for our rehearsal dinner. She firmly believed containing Anarchy's parents in a venue of her choosing was a wise decision.

I thought taking Celeste and Oscar to the country club was like trying to douse a fire with gasoline.

When I'd pointed out the rehearsal dinner was usually the groom's family's responsibility, Mother barely contained her snort. "I'm not dining in that macrobiotic vegan place in the alternative church basement. We'll host at the club."

If Anarchy had his way, we'd have our rehearsal dinner at a BBQ joint or the fried chicken place on 87th.

Mother might eat BBQ or go to Stroud's, but not for her daughter's rehearsal dinner.

I tried not to think about Celeste explaining the patriarchy to the waitresses at the club and tamped down my nerves at meeting Anarchy's father.

We tipped Becky and Marla and walked to the salon's doors. "I'm fairly certain Anarchy's family will hate me."

Karma frowned. "Hate you?"

"They despise authority, distrust the government, and drink wheatgrass shakes for breakfast. Anarchy's father teaches a class on Che Guevara. His mother thinks I am a meat-eating, country-club-attending Midwesterner."

Karma's lips twitched.

"And she's right."

"And her son is hopelessly in love with you. He'd scale mountains, slay dragons, endure Frances."

By marrying me, Anarchy was signing himself up for a challenging mother-in-law.

"Are his siblings coming?" she asked.

"Yes." I swallowed a golf ball of unease. "He seldom talks about them."

"Anarchy's the rebel of the family," said Karma, who knew my fiancé from college.

"Really?" Anarchy's rebellion came in the form of strict adherence to the rule of law, a possibly misguided belief in government, and a penchant for plaid sports coats.

Karma offered me a sympathetic wince. "Be warned, Journey will probably insist on singing Joan Baez at your wedding reception."

"As long as it's not 'Love is Just a Four-Letter Word.'" I swallowed a second golf ball. "What about River?"

"He runs deep."

"Very funny."

"But also true. You'll see when you meet him."

CHAPTER EIGHT

Three trucks sat in the circle drive in front of my house. Three. And I'd hoped to come home to a modicum of peace. It was not to be.

I parked at the curb and rested my forehead against the steering wheel. Maybe, rather than go inside, I'd find an anonymous bar, drink an anonymous martini, and return in an hour when the florist and his army had disappeared.

So cowardly. So tempting.

I closed my eyes and conjured a vision of a mahogany bar, wooden stools, and a barkeep named Mae. Mae mixed a mean martini, listened better than a shrink, and kept her patrons' secrets. I imagined bowls of questionable Spanish peanuts, stale cigarette smoke, and cheap ashtrays. The place was a dream come true. Especially if Anarchy joined me there.

Tap, tap.

I jerked away from the wheel.

Tap, tap.

Marian Dixon, my across-the-street neighbor, stood at the car window. She wore a floral housedress and a pinched expression.

I lowered the window. "Good afternoon, Marian."

"Your gardeners spilled mulch in the street in front of my house." She pointed at a trail of mulch.

Was she kidding? I studied her humorless expression. Not kidding.

"It needs to be swept."

I could argue or refuse (which would invite an argument). Instead, I chose the path most likely to return her to her home. "I'll clean it up."

"I don't want you to clean it up." A frown creased her forehead, and her lips pinched.

"Then why point it out?"

"I want you to call your lawn company. They should clean it up."

Oh dear Lord. The mulch would be gone by morning, but until a string of cars scattered the bits of shredded bark and woodchips, Marian would relentlessly demand its removal.

There were certain absolute truths in the universe. Gravity. Newton's law. Murphy's law. And that the garden center would not send a crew to sweep spilled mulch. "I'll clean it up."

"If you don't call, they'll do it again."

"I'm sure it was an accident."

"Are you?" Her narrowed eyes screamed conspiracy.

"Marian, why would they purposefully spill mulch in front of your house?"

"My yard looks better than the ones they manage."

Marian obsessed over her neighbors' comings and goings and her lawn. Grace swore she'd come home from a date last fall and seen Marian raking while wearing a lighted miner's helmet. She picked fights with snowplow drivers who dumped too much snow on her easement. She came close to cardiac arrest whenever a dog lifted its leg near her grass.

I swallowed a retort—one that included thoughts on the barren wasteland of a life spent measuring the length of grass blades and monitoring her neighbors. "I'll call." No way, no how was I calling about spilled mulch. "If they can't come today?"

She frowned.

"It's late in the day. And it's Friday. They may not make it here till Monday."

Marian's frown deepened.

"Then what?" I insisted.

Deep furrows lined her forehead and her hands clenched into fists. Not forcing the lawn service's return late on a Friday afternoon obviously pained her. "Fine. You clean it up. But if it happens again, I'm calling my lawyer."

"I'm sorry this upset you." I gripped the wheel with how sorry I wasn't. Not even a little bit. But I forced a smile. Marian was a neighbor, and I didn't want to start a feud over mulch.

"I'll give you twenty minutes."

I bit back a decidedly unneighborly response.

Marian tapped her watch.

I turned off the car, fetched a broom and dustpan from the garage, and wheeled the trash bin we used for yard waste to the curb. Then I stepped into the street.

Marian stood on her front stoop and supervised with her arms crossed.

I tamped the urge to toss the mulch into her yard, bent my head, and swept.

The roar of a car engine had me jumping to the curb. A teenage boy raced by, trailing exhaust and "Sympathy for the Devil."

When the car turned at the corner, I returned to the street, reswept the scattered mulch, and crouched to pick up the neat pile before the next car scattered it.

"Ellison, what on earth are you doing?" Mother's outraged voice straightened my spine. She sat in the passenger seat of Daddy's Mercedes, and I stared into her horrified eyes.

"Good afternoon." I checked my watch. "Good evening."

"Why are you cleaning the street?"

"The lawn service spilled mulch in front of Marian's house."

"Why isn't Marian cleaning it up?"

"My lawn service."

Mother tsked. "Why would they mulch beds the day before your wedding?"

Mulch smelled. And the wedding was on the patio.

Where had they added mulch?

I dumped the contents of the dustpan, dragged the waste bin to the bottom of the drive, grabbed my handbag from my unlocked car, and headed toward the backyard.

"Where are you going?" Mother demanded.

I cast a disbelieving look over my shoulder. "To find the mulch."

Daddy parked behind my car, and Mother opened her door. "Maybe this is a sign. Postpone."

"Mulch is not a sign." I shook off Mother's doubts and disapproval. I charged up the driveway.

The rumble from the waste bin's wheels followed behind me. Daddy had taken pity on me and was dragging it to the garage.

I flashed a smile over my shoulder then pushed open the gate to the backyard.

The florist had transformed the back patio. Lush ferns and blue hydrangeas in white porcelain pots crowded its edges. At the patio's back end stood an ivy-covered arch. My wrought-iron furniture was gone, replaced by neat rows of white wooden chairs.

"Oh," I breathed.

Mother, who'd followed me, sniffed.

"You can't possibly find fault with this. It's gorgeous."

"It's lovely." The admission sounded painful. She scowled at the archway as if it were covered in poison, not English ivy. "You know, it's not too late to change your mind."

This again? "Did your mother give you this talk before you married Daddy?" Because I sure hadn't heard it prior to marrying Henry.

"All I ever wanted for you was marriage to the right man."

"That's *all* you wanted for me?" Just a man. No career. No personal success. Just a man. Nope. That was wrong. Not just a man. It had to be the right man.

I'd married the right man, and he'd made me so miserable I'd found an outlet and a career that helped define my life.

"The man and the lifestyle that comes with him." Mother conveniently ignored the core truth of my question. She believed I needed a man for protection and security and status. "I wish you'd found someone more like Henry."

"You saw how that worked out."

Her nostrils flared. "If you're going to be difficult, I'll find the mulch. I bet they left it too close to the patio." She stepped off the bricks, walked four steps into the grass, and shrieked.

I clutched my heart and jumped three feet in the air.

Aggie appeared in the back door. Daddy came running.

"Frannie." He stared at his unmolested wife who shrieked loud enough to reanimate the bodies I'd found this week. "What happened?"

She lifted a foot. "Is this from a dog or an elephant?" The glare she cast my way could melt skin from bone. "How does a single animal make such an unholy mess?"

The unholy mess covered the bottom of Mother's shoe and oozed up the sides. It also smelled. The odor was nausea inducing. What were we feeding Max?

"Don't just stand there," she snapped. "Do something."

Daddy raced into the breach and claimed her elbow.

Aggie stepped onto the patio with a roll of paper towels.

Max, the responsible party, remained hidden in the house. He was smart that way.

I kept my mouth sealed for fear the giggle that was tickling my throat might escape.

Mother, with Daddy's help, stepped backward, away from Max's attempt to fertilize the lawn. She stepped out of her shoe and gave melting my skin from my bones a second try (if at first you don't succeed...).

"I'm sorry, Mother." My voice was reedy. "I hired a service to clean the backyard. That must be fresh."

"You think?"

Aggie made a choking sound, almost as if she'd swallowed a laugh. Not helping.

"The shoes are dyed to match the suit, Ellison. And they're ruined. What do you propose I do?"

"I'll replace them."

"Doesn't do me much good tonight." Gathering her outraged dignity around her like an ermine cloak, Mother gave Daddy a pointed look. "Harrington, I need to change clothes. We have to go home."

Daddy was too smart to argue. "Of course, dear. I'll bring the car up."

He left me with Mother, who vibrated with righteous indignation, and Aggie, who clutched the paper towels like a life preserver.

"Mother—" I forced back a giggle that might incite murder "—I'm so sorry about this."

"It's a sign," she decreed. "Don't get married."

"You stepping in dog doo is a sign?"

She nodded.

"I don't think so."

"It certainly is. This whole thing is a shit idea."

Wow. My eyes filled with tears, but my spine stiffened.

"Frannie." Daddy had pulled up the car, and he stood at the patio's edge. "That's enough. It's Ellison's life. She loves him. He loves her. Let it be."

Mother sniffed, abandoned her ruined shoe, and hobbled toward him.

"I'm happy, Mother. I wish you'd be happy for me."

We stared at each other for long seconds, then Mother gave a slight nod of her chin. "It's your life." That was as close to a blessing as I could hope for. Of course, it might also be a curse.

When they pulled out of the drive, I turned to Aggie. "Where's the florist?" Surely with three trucks in the drive there should be workers.

"He and his staff came inside for fresh cookies and went out the front door." That or they'd heard Mother's screech and run for the hills.

We glanced at Mother's ruined shoe.

"I'll deal with that," said Aggie. "You pour yourself a glass of wine."

"Thank you." I stepped into the kitchen, shot Max one of Mother's melt-the-skin-off-your-bones glares, dropped my purse on the counter, and opened the fridge.

Brnng, brnng.

I scowled at the phone.

It's rung all day. Mr. Coffee's smile was apologetic. *You have ten million messages.*

Brnng, brnng.

I picked up the phone. "Russell residence."

"Ellison? It's Laura Gilchrist. Am I catching you at a bad time?"

Totally. I wedged the receiver between my ear and shoulder and splashed wine into a glass. "Not at all."

"I called to see how you're feeling."

"Fine." Overwhelmed. The rehearsal started in less than an hour, and Mother's ruined shoe guaranteed she'd spend the evening being as pleasant as a grizzly awakened in January.

"Finding Lilly must have been so terrible for you."

Lilly. I was a horrible person. I'd found three bodies this

week (the number was high, even for me) and I was thinking of mulch and the dog doo on Mother's shoe. "Thank you for thinking of me. Were you and Lilly close?"

"She was a good neighbor." Laura let a full five seconds pass, then added, "You know how she was."

Lilly had a reputation as a social climber. *Human milkweed,* Mother called her.

Laura's silence spun like a 45 record on Grace's turntable.

I sipped my wine and waited.

"No good comes from speaking ill of the dead," Laura murmured.

Lilly had been a grasping, ambitious woman, dissatisfied with her country club and the couples in her supper club. When her daughters were in grade school, she selected their friends. When the girls went to high school, she screened their dates for pedigree, not character. No one was surprised when the girls went away to college and found husbands from the coasts. "You're right," I agreed.

Grace burst through the back door. "The patio looks amazing." Her backpack thunked onto the kitchen floor. "It's magical out there." She noticed the phone attached to my ear and mouthed, "Sorry."

"Laura, I must run. Thanks so much for calling."

"Best wishes to you."

We hung up, and I gave Grace my full attention.

"Sorry, I didn't realize you were on the phone."

I waved aside her apology. "You gave me a reason to hang up."

"The patio," she murmured.

"Do you like it?"

"Are you kidding? It's gorgeous. What does the rest of the house look like?"

"I haven't checked." With my refilled wine glass firmly

gripped in my right hand, I followed Grace to the foyer, where pots of hyacinths perfumed the air. Pot after cobalt-and-white-Chinese-porcelain pot filled the space. Dragons dazzled. Blossoms bloomed. Blue tigers stalked through indigo bamboo. Cerulean horses pranced with azure birds.

"I bet heaven smells like this." Grace held out her arms and spun in a circle.

"You might be right." I peeked into the living room and gasped.

Delphinium, blue hyacinths, and hydrangeas rubbed blossoms with white roses and English stock. They filled crystal vases of every size and shape and covered every surface.

"It's stunning," said Grace.

I nodded my agreement.

From the living room, we went to the dining room, where a breathtaking arrangement sat in the center of the table. Someone had shifted the small buffet table from the wall and draped it with my grandmother's lace tablecloth. Tomorrow it would hold a cake.

"It's perfect." Grace wiped her eyes with the back of her hand.

"Honey, are you crying?"

"What? Me? No." She offered me a watery smile. "I'm so happy for you."

I stared at the lovely girl standing in front of me. Her skin glowed with the beginning of her summer tan. Her curved lips revealed perfect teeth (thanks to years of orthodontia). Her eyes sparkled. This beautiful young woman was my daughter. My heart cracked with love, and I opened my arms.

She stepped into my embrace.

"I'm so proud of you," I whispered into her glossy hair.

She tightened her arms around my waist. "You deserve this, Mom. You deserve happiness."

Seconds passed as I willed myself not to cry. "I know you miss your dad."

"I do. I always will. But the two of you were terrible together." No need to elaborate on the disaster that was my first marriage. "Daddy made you cry. Anarchy makes you smile. Every day."

"He does."

The front door opened and my groom stepped inside. He looked at Grace and me, still clasped together. "Am I interrupting?"

We separated, and I went to him and kissed his cheek. "Not at all. I'm glad you're home. How was your day?"

He stiffened.

"That bad?"

"We should talk."

"That's adult speak for 'get lost, kid.'" Grace spun on her heel and returned to the kitchen.

Dread settled in my stomach. Had Anarchy changed his mind about marrying me? I searched his face for a clue. Same coffee-brown eyes. Same lean lines. Same delicious lips. Surely if he were about to dump me, I'd see it on his face. I gathered my courage and asked, "What's wrong?"

"How close are you to Tori Parks and Dot Thompson?"

I blinked. He wanted to talk about murder? Relief so strong it wobbled my knees flooded through me.

Anarchy caught my elbow and steadied me. His brows drew together. "Ellison?"

"Sorry. I'm fine. When you said we needed to talk, I thought you'd changed your mind."

"About?"

"Marrying me."

He barked a laugh. "Are you kidding? I'm the luckiest man on the planet." His arms drew me close till my nose bumped his chest.

I tilted my head and looked into his eyes.

"You might have noticed, I can be a bit—" the muscles in his handsome face tightened "—rigid. Once I pick a path, I don't deviate. I love you. I always will."

I blinked back tears and rested my cheek against the fabric of his summer-weight wool suit. "So," I spoke around the thickness in my throat, "what about Tori and Dot?"

"They lied about their alibi."

That was bad. "How do you know?"

"The manager of the store next to the thrift shop remembers seeing them there."

"He's sure?"

"He described Dot's car. Even remembered the license plate."

That was very bad. "Why?"

"The man has a thing for Mercedes 280SLs. Dot drives a red one. He saw it in the parking lot."

"Which parking lot?"

"In front of the thrift shop."

"The killer came through the back."

"She lied, Ellison. So did Tori."

"It has to be unrelated. I can't see either of them killing Avery." Becky's words came back to me.

"What?" Anarchy's hands tightened around my arms.

"My manicurist gossips."

"Everyone you know gossips."

"That's not fair."

"What did the manicurist say?"

"Avery said one of the Stallard children tried to get around her, but she'd turned the tables and got the best of them." That sounded pretty damning when Avery ended up dead. "I still think Dot and Tori are innocent."

"And Paige?"

I forced a smile. "I need to change. People will be arriving shortly."

"I have to tell Peters."

"I know." I pulled free of his arms and headed toward the stairs. "Can we let Peters handle this?"

"Of course." He flashed me a grin. "I have other things to do."

CHAPTER NINE

"You're breathtaking." Anarchy's whispered breath tickled my ear.

"You have to say that. You're marrying me." I tilted my chin and looked up into his sparkling brown eyes. "And you look very handsome." Handsome was too pale a word. In his navy suit, crisp white shirt, and red tie, Anarchy made my blood fizz like Champagne.

He smoothed his lapel and offered me a self-conscious grin. "Your mother narrows her eyes when I wear plaid jackets."

Mother and Daddy stood on the other side of the living room, where she supervised Daddy's bartending. Straight gin in a martini glass. That meant Mother was still furious.

There was a time when Mother's ire gave me heart palpitations, when I did anything and everything to appease her. No longer. I'd offered to buy her new shoes. And it was an accident. But Frances Walford made a point of holding her anger close, like a mother with a newborn baby.

I frowned. Tomorrow, I'd marry the man of my dreams, and she'd rather nurse a grudge than enjoy the weekend.

Watching the haughty tilt of her chin, I vowed to never, ever punish Grace with cold anger.

Ding, dong.

Anarchy's gaze shifted to the foyer, where Aggie hurried toward the front door.

"Finally," he muttered.

His family was late.

Just the thought of meeting Anarchy's father made my palms sweat, made my heart beat like a kettle drum, made my mouth go dry. We should have gone to the hotel to welcome the Joneses to Kansas City. Then I wouldn't have to make my father-in-law's acquaintance at my wedding rehearsal.

Aggie opened the front door, and a single man stepped into my home.

Next to me, Anarchy stiffened.

Aggie closed the door.

Anarchy's jaw firmed, and he strode into the foyer.

I followed behind him. Slowly. I needed a moment to assess the stranger who would soon be my brother-in-law. River Jones was tall and lean like Anarchy, but his eyes were the blue of faded denim. He wore a dove gray suit, a pale blue shirt, and a rep tie. His lips were fuller than Anarchy's. Almost pouty. They gave his thin face a spoiled air.

Where were their parents? Their sister?

I held out my right hand. "You must be River. I'm Ellison."

"A pleasure." River's handshake was firm. And damp. Was he as nervous as I was?

"We're so glad you're here."

The corner of Anarchy's left eye twitched as if it were keeping time with a Mariachi band.

"You came alone?" Worse than meeting Anarchy's father was knowing he didn't want to meet me.

A shadow passed over River's face, and he nodded.

"Where are Mom and Dad?"

"They'll join us for dinner." River didn't sound convinced they'd actually show. "Journey, too."

Anarchy growled.

I rested my hand on his arm. We couldn't shoot the messenger. "Wonderful." I tried for an isn't-that-fabulous tone, but that *wonderful* sank faster than a lead balloon. "I can't wait to see them. I haven't met your father or Journey."

River blinked like an owl in noon-day sun. "I hear you're a painter."

As transitions went, it was incredibly awkward. I tamped down my they-don't-want-to-meet-me disappointment and forced a smile. "I am."

"A successful artist," said Anarchy.

River's answering grin was stiff.

"Mom?"

Our gazes shifted to Grace. She wore a Lilly Pulitzer shift (blue pandas, green jungle, white background) and chunky blue sandals. On seeing her, Mother had deemed the outfit too casual and sent her upstairs to change. Instead, with my blessing, Grace had escaped to help Aggie in the kitchen (at the rate Aggie was cooking for the reception, we'd have enough canapés to feed an army).

Grateful for the interruption, I beckoned. "Come meet Anarchy's brother. River, this is my daughter, Grace."

The two shook hands. Then Grace asked, "Where are Professor and Mrs. Jones?"

The brothers had twin tics near their left eyes.

"They've decided to join us at dinner."

Grace frowned. "But the rehearsal—"

"We'll manage without them." My voice was sharper than I intended, but who could blame me? My future in-laws thought so little of me they'd skipped our wedding rehearsal. Mother would have a field day with this. I glanced over my shoulder into the living room, where Mother had downed her martini.

She watched Daddy make another one, then shifted her gaze my way, as if she sensed my dismay like a shark sensed blood in the water.

"Grace." Anarchy nodded toward the living room. "Would you please introduce River to your grandparents?"

For a moment I thought she'd argue—or run for the hills. Mother was sure to ask after the rest of the Joneses. And unlike me, she shot messengers. "Of course." Grace sounded like shims under her fingernails were a better alternative, but she did as he asked.

When River and Grace stepped away, Anarchy's hand circled my wrist. "A word?" He led me into the dining room and scowled at the blameless floral arrangement on the table. He released me, held his hands in front of his face, flexed his fingers, then clenched them into tight fists. He tapped a fist against his narrowed lips. He said nothing. His body did the talking. The stiffness of his neck and shoulders. The fire in his eyes. The near-tangible anger that rose from his skin. He was so furious he couldn't speak.

"Don't worry about it."

"Don't worry?" The gravel in his voice rumbled through me.

"Compared to the things Mother has said to you, skipping a rehearsal is nothing."

He winced.

"And don't count on her getting better after we're married," I warned. "She'll be emboldened." I shuddered to think of the arrows she'd sling.

"Your mother says those things because she loves you."

"Being a mother shouldn't give a person leave to eviscerate her daughter." I smiled at Anarchy. "Or her daughter's fiancé. Or her daughter's husband."

"We're talking about my parents, not yours."

"Fair enough. All I'm saying is if you can forgive Mother's jibes, I can forgive your parents' absence."

He pulled me close, and I rested my forehead against his chest.

His arms circled my waist. "You're not mad?"

"It's not ideal." Such an understatement. "But compared to finding a body, this is but a bump in the road."

Ding, dong.

Enclosed in the safety of his arms, I was loath to move.

"Aggie can get that." Anarchy's hold on me tightened—as if he too dreaded dealing with our families.

Seconds passed.

Ding, dong.

"Aggie must be busy in the kitchen," I said.

"Then Grace." He obviously didn't know teenagers. If I wanted Grace to open the door, I'd have to ask. And to ask, I'd have to go to the living room. And if I was in the front hall on my way to the living room, I might as well answer the door.

Additional seconds passed without the sound of anyone answering the door.

I sighed and pulled free. "I'd better get that. It might be Reverend Phillips."

"Or Libba."

"Could be," I allowed. "But this is too close to being on time. Maybe your parents changed their minds."

Anarchy didn't bother with a reply. Together we walked to the front door, and I pulled it open.

Reverend Phillips waited on the stoop. The man was ridiculously tall and rangy, with a mop of graying hair and twinkling eyes.

"Welcome," I told him. "We're so glad you're here."

He responded with a kind smile. "I'm honored you asked me to officiate."

"Please." I stood to the side. "Come in."

The reverend and Mother entered the foyer at the same instant.

"Grayson." She stepped forward and offered her cheek for a kiss. "We're so grateful to you."

"My pleasure, Frances."

Mother clutched her martini glass as if she'd decided the only way to survive the weekend was with copious amounts of gin and an olive or two thrown in for fun. "If you'll step into the living room, Harrington will fix you a drink. We can't start without the maid of honor." Mother cut her gaze at me as if I were responsible for Libba's tardiness.

Mother led Reverend Phillips toward a Tom Collins.

"In less than two days, we'll be on a plane to Italy." Anarchy's whispered words were a hope, a promise, a lifeline.

Was that why people went on honeymoons? The carrot for surviving a wedding. "We should have eloped," I murmured.

Anarchy's face clouded. He was the one who'd wanted a wedding with our families. I suspected the tradition appealed to him. But rather than support him, his parents had made this evening awkward. Then there was Mother. One more martini, and she'd be drunk. "I should have listened to you. If I had, you'd already be my wife."

Anger at Mother and Anarchy's parents bubbled in my chest. "This—" and by *this*, I meant both Mother's martinis and the Joneses' cruel absence "—doesn't matter." My hand closed over the taut arm muscles hidden by his suit. "Nothing matters, not as long as we end up married."

Ding, dong.

Since we were already in the foyer, I yanked open the door.

"Were you waiting on the other side?" Libba made a show of glancing at her watch. "I'm not that late." Her other arm remained hidden behind her back. She glanced over her shoulder and called, "Charlie, are you coming?"

Charlie listed to the left from the weight of a scuffed case. He walked next to a woman in a mauve chiffon dress.

"What is Charlie carrying, and who is that?" I demanded.

"A harp. And that's the harpist."

I stared at the woman, whose flesh threatened to erupt from the frilly chiffon. "What harpist?"

Libba's grin was both sly and amused. "You didn't hire a harpist?"

"I did not."

"Frances strikes again?"

I reached for Anarchy's hand. "Could we leave tonight? Get married in Venice?

"No you don't." Libba thrust a bow bouquet at me. "This is my chance to be your maid of honor and you can't spoil it for me."

I gazed at the bouquet. "You did this?" She'd strung bows through a paper plate. The ribbons were crushed, and their ends trailed, but a lump rose in my throat.

"I did my best." She sounded defensive. "I saved the bows from the shower."

"It's perfect." I hugged her. Tightly. "Thank you."

"You're welcome. Is everyone here?" She glanced around the foyer, ready to count noses. "Where's Max?"

"Upstairs in my bedroom. It's better if Mother doesn't see him tonight."

Charlie stepped inside, kissed my cheek, shook Anarchy's hand, and nodded at the woman whose case he carried. "You've met Gayla?"

"Haven't had the pleasure."

"But you—"

"Mother hired her." I extended my hand to the harpist, whose only sin was being hired by Mother. "I'm Ellison and this is my fiancé, Anarchy."

Gayla stared at Anarchy as if she'd never seen a man before. The gaze went on and on.

Libba giggled.

Charlie pulled on his collar.

Anarchy's expression, bland and polite, didn't change.

It was up to me to break the spell. "The rehearsal is on the patio. I'll show you the way."

"I can carry this out for you," Charlie offered.

"I can carry it." Gayla reclaimed her case.

Each of them tugged at the handle.

"Charlie, would you please get me a drink?" asked Libba.

He immediately relinquished the harp case. "What'll it be?"

Libba raised her brows. "Need you ask?"

"A martini," said Charlie. "Extra dirty."

"Exactly." Libba smiled her approval. "I'll go with Ellison, show Gayla where to set up, and see you in a minute."

"This way." I took a step toward the back of the house, and Gayla followed me.

We passed through the kitchen, where Aggie raised a who's-that brow, and stepped onto the patio.

"It's lovely out here," said Gayla.

"She's right," Libba agreed. "It's gorgeous."

"The florist. I take no credit. Gayla, we'll let you set up. We should begin soon."

Gayla nodded and opened her case. Inside was a harp she could hold on her lap.

Libba and I returned to the house. She grabbed my wrist and stopped me from leaving the kitchen. "I heard you found Lilly Frasier."

"I did."

"That makes three this week."

"Who's counting?"

"Frances."

I winced. She was one hundred percent right. Mother was counting.

"Poor Lilly."

To my knowledge, Libba had no use for Lilly. I raised my brows.

"She finally got what she wanted, then she drowned."

"What do you mean?" I asked.

"Lilly told Billie Weston that she and her husband were being proposed for membership at the country club."

My jaw dropped. "Our country club? By whom?" I sounded starchy.

"You could be Frances right now."

Was I becoming my mother? "Don't be mean."

"So Lilly did some social climbing." Libba dismissed decades of backbiting and using people with a small shake of her shoulders. "It wasn't as if she killed people or cheated at bridge."

"She wasn't a nice woman."

"There are plenty of awful women at the club."

My brows rose to my hairline.

"Prudence." Libba said the name as if the mere mention proved her point.

"True." I hated to cede, but Prudence Davies defined awful.

"Come on." She tugged my arm. "I need that martini. And it looks to me like you need one, too."

We returned to a quiet living room.

Mother stared into her martini, as if the olive at the bottom of the glass had the power to cancel weddings or turn a recalcitrant daughter into a biddable one.

Anarchy and River glared at each other.

Grace and Charlie huddled on opposite corners of the couch.

And Daddy and Reverend Phillips wore crestfallen expressions, as if they'd unexpectedly survived Mother's outburst and weren't sure that was a good thing.

Mother looked up from her drink. "I understand your new in-laws decided to skip the rehearsal."

"Yes."

She hiccupped. "This doesn't concern you?"

I glanced at Anarchy, whose face was unreadable. "It does not."

"Then you're a fool."

Anarchy winced.

"That's enough, Mother." What had she said in my absence? "Reverend, I believe we're ready to begin. The logistics are simple. Our parents will be seated, then Libba and River will walk down the aisle."

Libba waggled her fingers at River.

"Then Grace will give me away."

Mother made a sound like a wounded animal.

"Shall we?" I waved toward the hallway that led to the patio.

"Come along, Frances." Daddy claimed Mother's elbow.

She hiccupped. "Fine. But I need another drink."

No one was brave enough to tell her she'd had enough, so Daddy poured her another martini.

We relocated to the flower-filled patio, where the harpist strummed soothing chords.

Mother sighted Gayla's dress and narrowed her eyes. "Ellison, who is that?"

"Gayla."

"Who?"

"The harpist you hired." Without consulting me.

She frowned. "I didn't realize she dressed like that. You'll need to tell her what to wear tomorrow."

No one would care what the harpist wore.

"If we could begin?" Reverend Phillips checked his watch.

Daddy escorted Mother down the short aisle, then Charlie stood in for the Joneses.

Libba pressed the bow bouquet into my hands and accepted River's arm.

The two walked down the aisle, then split apart in front of the archway, where Anarchy waited with Reverend Phillips.

"Our turn." Grace offered me a warm smile.

"What did your grandmother say in the living room?"

"Trust me." Her smile faded. "You don't want to know. Are you ready?"

More than ready.

Grace walked me down the aisle, put my hand in Anarchy's, and kissed our cheeks.

I gave Libba the bow bouquet and turned my attention to the minister.

"Dearly beloved, we have come together in the presence of God to witness and bless the joining together of this man and this woman in holy matrimony."

Mother snorted.

Reverend Phillips glanced her way, paled, lost his place in the prayer book, cleared his throat, and said, "The union of husband and wife in heart, body, and mind is intended by God for their mutual joy, for the help and comfort given to one another in prosperity and adversity, and, when it is God's will, for the procreation of children and their nurture in the knowledge and love of the Lord."

Mother muttered something decidedly un-Christian.

I glared at her.

"Into this holy union Ellison and Anarchy now come to be joined. If any of you can show just cause why they may not lawfully be married, speak now, or else forever hold your peace."

I tensed.

Everyone watched Mother, waiting for her to pull out a list.

She slurped her martini.

"Ellison, will you have this man to be your husband, to live together in the covenant of marriage? Will you love him, comfort him, honor and keep him, in sickness and in health, and forsaking all others, be faithful to him as long as you both shall live?"

"I will."

Mother listed to the side.

"Anarchy, will you have this woman to be your wife, to live together in the covenant of marriage? Will you love her, comfort her, honor and keep her, in sickness and in health, and forsaking all others, be faithful to her as long as you both shall live?"

"I will."

"Will all of you witnessing these promises do all in your power to uphold these two persons in their marriage?"

Mother belched and fell off her chair.

CHAPTER TEN

"I'm grateful your parents aren't here to see this."

Grateful was too pale a word. I was get-down-on-my-knees, offer-my-first-born thankful.

Anarchy's lips quirked, and he squeezed my hand. Together, we watched Daddy and Charlie half-walk, half-drag Mother toward the kitchen and Mr. Coffee's magical elixir.

I peeked at River, who tracked Mother's progress with a horrified expression on his face.

"You two can't ever divorce," said Libba

I scowled at my friend. Anarchy and I weren't yet married, and she was already talking about divorce. "Pardon me?" I added a healthy dose of frost to my voice.

She ignored the chill. "For as long as you're married, you can tell this story at holiday dinners, family brunches, reunions. Frances will rue that fifth martini for the rest of her life."

I couldn't help but grin.

Reverend Phillips stared at the gate to the driveway as if he were considering a quick escape. He caught me watching, gulped, and pulled on his collar. "Shall we finish?"

"Please," Anarchy replied.

"You'll complete the vows." Apparently, the reverend had decided on the abbreviated version. Not a bad idea. "You'll kiss the bride. I'll introduce you as Mr. and Mrs. Jones. Then you'll walk up the aisle together. Your maid of honor and best man will follow."

Typical wedding. Nothing new. "Thank you, Reverend Phillips, and I apologize for the disruption."

His answering smile was kind. "Emotions run high at weddings. They're worse than funerals that way."

My brows lifted.

"Everyone knows funerals call for sadness," he explained. "If the congregants feel anything but sorrow or sympathy, they hide it. Weddings? You get love and happiness and jealousy and worry and spite and pettiness and—"

"We get the picture." Anarchy scowled at his brother as if River were responsible for their parents' absence.

Tomorrow would overflow with the emotions the reverend had mentioned. Love and happiness (hopefully what most of us would feel). Jealousy (my sister, Marjorie, who demanded the world revolve around her). Worry (Mother and Daddy). Spite (hopefully no one would be spiteful). Pettiness (Marjorie? Anarchy's family? Mother?).

I lifted my chin and focused on love and happiness. And with Anarchy in front of me, that was easy. My forehead rested briefly on his chest, then I tilted my head and stared into his eyes.

"One more day," he murmured, as if he'd read my mind.

"One," I echoed.

He leaned in and kissed me. The kiss was chaste, but my toes curled inside my shoes.

Libba chucked. "Ellison, you're blushing." I ignored her and lifted my hand to Anarchy's cheek.

"Mooooommmm." Long. Drawn out. Overflowing with teenage my-mother-is-so-embarrassing angst.

"Why don't you two go check on Mother?" I spoke from the side of my mouth.

"We don't have a death wish," Libba replied.

And death waited for anyone who followed Mother. It was a shame about Grace. She had her whole life ahead of her—but Libba deserved her fate. "I'm getting married tomorrow." I couldn't follow Mother, couldn't die today.

"You're the only one strong enough to stand up to her," Libba countered.

I turned my head away from my perfect husband-to-be and blinked. Repeatedly. "Me?" Had she lost her mind?

"You," she confirmed. "Or hadn't you noticed?"

I had not. Mother had spent nearly forty years pushing me around. It was only in the past year that I'd learned to draw a line in the sand.

Libba shifted her gaze to Anarchy. "Frances blames you for Ellison's new independence, but she's wrong. It's all Ellison. She finally grew a pair."

Reverend Phillips guffawed.

Grace giggled.

River laughed out loud.

Anarchy grinned.

And I considered what Libba said. Was she right? I still let Mother have her way for small things, like the location for the rehearsal dinner. But when it came to important things, I stood my ground.

Anarchy tugged at my left hand. "We'll check on her together."

I paused and extended my right hand. "Thank you for being here, Reverend Phillips. Will you be joining us at the rehearsal dinner?"

"I need to rest up for the wedding. I'll see you tomorrow." His eyes twinkled, and I strongly suspected he was avoiding drama.

Anarchy tugged again, and we headed inside and found Charlie alone. Mother and Daddy were gone.

"Where did they go?" I demanded.

"Your father took your mother home." Charlie offered me an apologetic grimace. "He says he'll meet you at the club."

"They left?" I didn't mean to sound forlorn, but my voice was as wilted as dying flowers.

"He said your mother needed a rest."

My mother was three sheets, but I needed her.

Anarchy's hand clasped my waist, and he pulled me close to his side. "You okay?"

Keep your chin up. Mr. Coffee offered me a supportive smile. *You can handle anything the Joneses can dish out.*

Could I? I tamped down unexpected hurt and burgeoning panic. "Maybe this is for the best. Mother doesn't have a filter when she drinks. With too many martinis, there's no telling what she'd say." But I'd wanted her at my back when I faced Anarchy's family. She might be an iron-willed, take-no-prisoners bully, but she was my bully. And my mother. And I wanted her around for the special moments in my life.

"At least she showed up." Now Anarchy sounded forlorn.

I wrapped my arm around him and gave a comforting squeeze. Mother might have drank a gallon of gin, but his parents had skipped this moment. "Tonight is practice. Tomorrow, when it counts, everyone will be here. Sober." I'd make it happen. Mother had passed a bit of her iron will down, and I intended for Anarchy's and my wedding to be a slew of special moments. Each one shared with the people we loved.

Anarchy and I drove to the club together. Grace followed in her car, and Charlie and Libba gave River a ride.

As we pulled into the club's long, winding drive, he sighed.

"Long day?" I asked.

He rubbed the back of his neck. "Shouldn't we be talking about our future?"

"What does it say that your parents skipped our rehearsal?"

"The same as your mother getting drunk." That three out of four parents weren't happy for us.

I groaned. "What will we tell your parents about Mother?"

"The truth?"

"That my mother drank so much gin she needed to go home?"

"Maybe we tell them she's not feeling well."

I grinned. "Works for me. But River knows the truth."

"I'll talk to my brother. He won't say a word." Anarchy's hand wandered to my side of the car and claimed my fingers with a tight squeeze. "Also, whatever happens tonight, it's not our future. It's just our families behaving badly. Nothing more. Our future is nothing but happy."

"Promise?"

"Till death do us part."

We walked into the club holding hands. Paused in the entryway to the private dining room holding hands. Smiled at our friends and family holding hands.

Maybe it was a good thing Mother was at home. She abhorred public displays of affection, and in her mind hand holding was just that.

I disagreed.

My fingers laced with Anarchy's gave me strength and confidence. Their warmth made me feel cherished.

Aunt Sis and Gordon stepped forward, and she wrapped me in a hug. "You look beautiful, Ellison."

Gordon clapped Anarchy on the shoulder.

Aunt Sis released me and hugged Grace as she entered the room. My aunt nodded a welcome at Libba and Charlie, then returned her attention to me. "Where's Frances?"

I glanced at Anarchy. "Not feeling well."

Libba snorted, and Aunt Sis's brows rose.

I forced a smile. "Go with it." Then I opened my arms and

hugged Marjorie, who'd arrived at some point in the the afternoon.

"You're a bride." Her eyes glistened.

"I am."

"I'm happy for you." She was?

"I can't believe tomorrow I'll be Anarchy's wife."

Her gaze cut across the room to where Karma stood near the bar talking to Celeste and a man who must be Anarchy's father. The soft expression in Marjorie's eyes hardened to a diamond edge. "You invited Karma?"

"I did."

"If it makes you happy, I'm happy." Not words I ever expected from Marjorie. Especially not when she wore a sour pickles expression. It took a moment for the truth to dawn. Marjorie had decided to be a better, more supportive, more loving sister than Karma. I'd take what I could get.

I caught Anarchy's eye. "Want to introduce me to your dad?"

For a half-second, his face froze, and I sensed he wanted to run. Far. Fast. Away.

"Sure." He reclaimed my hand and walked me toward his parents with all the enthusiasm of a condemned man on his way to the gallows.

We stopped in front of them, and I gave Karma a quick hug, then forced my lips into a nervous smile. "Celeste." I pretended she smiled back. "How nice to see you."

She actually frowned and her brows drew together in an unhappy vee. "So you're really doing this?"

"Tomorrow." Anarchy's hand, already pressed against the small of my back, flexed. "Ellison, this is my father, Oscar Jones. Dad, meet my fiancée, Ellison Russell."

Oscar Jones looked like Anarchy and River, but his eyes were hard. No sparkle. No hint of friendliness. Just disapproval.

I thrust out my hand. "Nice to meet you, Mr. Jones."

My hand hung in space.

"Professor Jones," he corrected.

"Of course." I retracted my unshaken hand. "I apologize." I hadn't expected an encompassing hug from the man, but being snubbed by my future father-in-law hurt.

"Dad." Anarchy's tone matched the unpleasant expression in Oscar's eyes.

This was horrible—if-we-get-through-the-weekend-without-another-murder-it'll-be-a-miracle horrible. "I'm so sorry you couldn't join us at the rehearsal." I sounded like Mother right before she went in for the kill, sweet as strychnine-laced soda pop. And who could blame me? I could forgive his snub, but not the way he'd wounded Anarchy.

The air around us was as tense and sharp as a killer's blade.

"Mrs. Russell?" One of the waitstaff stood at my elbow.

I turned, and the young woman flushed. "You're needed in the kitchen."

I'd never received a call to the kitchen. "Pardon me?"

She shifted her weight from side to side and wrung her hands. "Please?"

"Of course." I excused myself from the awful interaction with Anarchy's parents (they glared at their son and he glared back) and followed her to the kitchen, where Chef looked ready to throw his best knives at a woman I didn't know.

His gaze shifted to me, and his face relaxed. Slightly. "Mrs. Russell, your guest..."

My guest? The dots connected. She wore a flowing peasant dress (should have been my first clue), and her brown hair flowed down her back and reached for her knees. Journey.

Anarchy's sister sized me up (wrap dress, manicured hands, arranged hair, and carefully applied lipstick, blush, and mascara), and sneered. Her own face was devoid of makeup. "You're serving meat." Her accusation hung in the air, mixed with the heady scent of roasting tenderloin.

"Yes."

"I'm a vegan."

"We arranged for grilled portobello mushrooms for your entrée."

"But you're serving meat."

"Most of our guests eat meat."

"My family doesn't."

Hence the meatless option. Dare I tell her that her brother's two favorite restaurants served fried chicken and BBQ? "Anarchy eats meat."

She gasped. "He does not."

"Ask him."

"I will." She brushed past me without another word. At least she'd left the kitchen.

"Sorry for the interruption, Chef."

"Sorry to pull you from your party, Mrs. Russell." He offered a shrug. "She wouldn't give up."

"Again, my apologies."

He'd already returned to his work. I turned on my heel. But rather than return to my party, my feet carried me to the ladies' lounge. I needed a moment to process Anarchy's family.

I settled on a stool at the long vanity and stared at the woman in the mirror. She was no longer young. But that wasn't a bad thing. With age came wisdom. I was smart enough to realize Anarchy's family would return to California. We could survive the weekend. Maybe.

When had my wedding become something to be survived?

At least we had an Italian honeymoon as our reward. And when we returned, Anarchy's family would be fifteen hundred miles away.

"Ellison?"

I shifted my thoughtful gaze and spotted Dot in the mirror. "Dot."

"You look lovely."

"Thank you. Rehearsal dinner."

"I have a confession."

My blood chilled. A confession? Oh dear Lord.

She bit into her lower lip. "Tori and I lied."

I blinked and turned so I looked at her, not her reflection. "What do you mean?"

"We lied about where we were the day Avery died."

Telling me after her alibi blew apart hardly inspired confidence. "Where were you?" I knew the answer, but would she finally tell the truth?

"The thrift shop."

"What happened?" I asked.

"Rose called us." She clasped her hands together. "Called me."

"Why?"

"We had a deal. She called whenever Avery donated Mom's things. We bought them before anyone put them on the sales floor."

"You had a backroom deal with Rose?" I closed my eyes and considered. No one would blame Dot or Tori for buying back their mother's belongings. "Why did you lie?"

"Because we had motive to kill Avery, and we were in the parking lot." The coincidence boggled the mind. "But we didn't kill her. You've got to believe me. You've got to tell your fiancé."

"It's not his case."

She waved aside my objection. "But he knows the detective."

I ceded her point with a nod. "When were you there?"

She squeezed her eyes shut. "Around four thirty. We waited for Rose to give us the all-clear, but she never did. You pulled into the parking lot, then the police, then we drove away."

They'd been in the parking lot while Rose and Avery were murdered. "Why are you telling me now?"

"We feel awful about lying." That or she and Tori knew another shop owner spotted them. "We were waiting for the all-clear from Rose," she repeated. "But rather than wave like she usually did, she shooed out a customer and locked the door."

"How many times did you buy things from Rose?"

"Two. Maybe three." She flushed. Was she lying again? "Always at the end of the day when Rose was there alone." Dot shifted her gaze to the carpet. "I'm not sure, but I suspect Rose was selling them to us directly."

"What do you mean?"

"Under the table."

I still didn't understand. I frowned.

"She didn't check the goods into inventory." Dot raised her gaze and spoke slowly, as if I weren't the sharpest crayon in the box. "She kept the money."

"When did this start?"

"In the last month or so. Please, Ellison, talk to your fiancé. This whole thing has been awful for Daddy. I can't put him through the shame of seeing his daughters arrested."

"I'll tell Anarchy what you told me."

"You believe me?"

"I do." Maybe. I rose from my bench. "I'll tell Anarchy we spoke, but right now I need to get to the dinner."

Approximately an hour later, Grace lifted her Champagne glass. Yes, she was underage. But this was a special, unique situation. She wanted to toast our happiness, and I wasn't about to stop her.

We needed Champagne and happiness after that dinner.

She cleared her throat and her cheeks flushed a light pink. "Mom, Anarchy." She raised her glass a bit higher. "I'm so happy for you both. Anarchy, my mother has smiled more in the past year than she did for the first fifteen years of my life. Thank you for that. And Mom, you may not remember, but when we first met Anarchy, he was a bit...rigid."

"Does that mean a stick-in-the mud, meat-eating rule follower?" Journey's question made Anarchy grimace.

"It means Anarchy has saved us, made us laugh, adopted a

cat, and filled my mother's life with over-the-moon joy," Grace replied.

Journey crossed her arms. Learning about Anarchy's taste for ribs and fried chicken had upset her deeply.

"The two of you are meant to be together," Grace continued. "Meant to be happy. Meant to extend my curfew till one a. m."

The room chuckled.

"Not happening, Grace."

She grinned. "You can't blame me for trying."

Anarchy squeezed my hand as Grace lifted her Champagne high. "Please raise your glasses to Mom and Anarchy. We wish you a lifetime of happiness."

CHAPTER ELEVEN

A deep growl had me levitating from my bed.

Grrr.

I wiped the sleep from my eyes. "What's wrong, Max?"

Grrr.

Moonlight spilling through the window revealed a ridge of fur standing straight on his back.

Fear made an appearance, leaned over, and whispered in my ear, "You're in trouble now."

I considered my options. Max didn't growl wolf. The rumble in his chest and throat meant something—an intruder, a body on the patio, a cat—was wrong.

I reached into my nightstand drawer and found the .22 I kept there. Feeling braver with a gun in my hand, I repeated my question. "What's wrong?"

Grrr.

He paced in front of the closed bedroom door. I'd followed Max and his midnight growls before. It never ended well. I definitely wasn't taking on whatever hid in the darkness the night before my wedding. I fumbled for the phone, dropped the receiver onto the bed, and dialed with my free hand.

Max stared at me with a slight sneer on his doggy lips, as if my new lack of bravery was a failing.

"Hello." Just the sound of Anarchy's voice calmed my frazzled nerves.

"Max is growling."

I could almost see Anarchy sit straighter, run an impatient hand through his hair, clench his free hand. "Are you safe?"

"I'm in my bedroom."

"And Grace?"

"She should be in hers. I'll check as soon as we hang up."

"I'm on my way."

"Thank you."

"You have your gun?"

"Yes."

"Keep it with you. Do not go downstairs."

Normally I bristled when a man told me what to do. But this was Anarchy, and he cared about our safety. "Promise."

"I'll be there in ten."

I hung up the phone, tiptoed into the hallway, and stopped in front of Grace's room.

Her door opened silently, and I peeked into her bedroom. She sprawled across her bed, her shoulders wedged between two teddy bears. She wore a ruffled nightie, and she'd shoved a daisy-covered blanket down to her waist. In sleep, she looked sweet and innocent and young, and I took a moment to listen to her steady breathing.

She was safe. And it would take a foghorn to wake her.

I backed into the hall, eased the door shut, and claimed a spot at the top of the stairs.

Max gave me a let's-catch-the-bad-guy look.

"I promised Anarchy I'd stay upstairs," I explained.

He rolled his eyes, then slinked down the stairs. He'd made no such promises.

"Max!" I whisper-yelled.

He glanced over his left shoulder, then continued to the first floor. He'd check the doors, maybe the windows, and attack any stranger.

What had I done to deserve tonight's interruption to my sleep? Usually when someone invaded my home, I had an inkling as to why. Not tonight. More accurately, not this morning. It was Saturday, the day Anarchy and I would exchange vows. My heart fluttered with happiness. Happiness I ignored. Right now, I had to worry about potential intruders.

"Max!" I whispered into the darkness.

My dog didn't respond.

Rather than raise my voice, I focused on controlling my heart rate.

I sat for an eternity while my ears strained to hear anything odd, and my eyes searched the darkness at the bottom of the stairs.

Where was Max? Where was Anarchy? Had ten minutes passed?

When I heard the front door open, I tensed.

"Ellison?" Anarchy's concerned voice bounded up the front stairs and wrapped me in its embrace.

"I'm here," I called. With the gun still clutched in my hand, I hurried down the stairs.

Anarchy waited in the foyer. The porch light shining through the open door cast his face in stark planes. "You're okay?"

I nodded and launched myself into his arms.

He hugged me. Tightly. Then gently pried the .22 from my fingers. "Max?"

"He's around here somewhere. Did you see anything?"

"Nope. Let's find him." He claimed my hand and led me toward the kitchen.

Max wasn't there.

We crept into the family room and spotted my dog. He stood in front of the French doors and stared fixedly into the backyard.

"Stay here." Anarchy left me at the room's entrance and joined Max by the French doors.

Max gave him an about-time-you-got-here look.

"Do you see anything?" I asked.

"No."

"What do we do?"

"Patrol car should be here any minute. They'll park in front for the night."

"The neighbors will love that." Anarchy didn't deserve my sarcasm, but I couldn't help the sass. Marian Dixon would have kittens over the cruiser. I pushed my hair away from my face. "And you? What will you do?"

"I'm staying."

A tight knot in my chest loosened. "You're not supposed to see me till the wedding."

He chuckled. "That ship sailed."

He was right. I joined him in front of the doors to the back yard. "What did you see, Max?"

Max settled on his haunches and yawned. Whatever the danger, it had passed.

I leaned against Anarchy. "I'm glad you're here."

"You're stuck with me."

Stuck was the last verb I'd use to describe being with Anarchy. "Likewise."

"Tonight when I close my eyes, you'll be my wife."

There it was—that extra flutter in my heart that spread to my stomach. "I'm so lucky."

He dropped a kiss on my head. "Pretty sure I'm the lucky one."

"You heard Grace. You reminded me how to smile."

"Well, you taught me how to live."

"Swoony words, Detective."

He grinned. "Swoony?"

"Go with it."

"If you say so." He stared into the darkness. "I'll check the yard with Max."

"And then?"

"Then bed. We have a big day."

SUNSHINE POURED through the kitchen windows, and I pushed Mr. Coffee's button.

Are you nervous?

"About Anarchy?" I'd left him asleep in our bed. "No. About the wedding? Definitely."

There were a million things that could go wrong. Our parents could fight. Journey could sing. The seams of whatever dress Gayla wore might fail.

Max rubbed his head against my leg. "Love you, buddy."

He yawned.

"Promise you'll behave tonight?" Neither of us enjoyed locking him in my bedroom.

His stubby tail twitched.

"I'll hold you to that. No sniffing crotches. No potty breaks near the patio. No chasing squirrels or barking like a lunatic."

His tail wagged like a metronome.

Coffee's ready.

Aside from *I love you* falling from Anarchy's lips, those were the sweetest words in the world.

I grabbed a mug and poured liquid perfection. "Thank you."

"Talking to the coffee maker?" Grace asked.

"You're up early." Deflection was the name of the game.

She merely grinned. "So what's the plan today?"

"Get married."

"That's at seven thirty. How are you spending the day? And don't tell me you plan on hanging out at home. You'll be in everyone's way."

"How about we go for breakfast?" Anarchy had snuck into the kitchen without us noticing.

"You shouldn't be here," said Grace.

Anarchy ran a hand through his hair. "Coffee?"

"Of course." I poured him a mug.

"Nuh-uh." Grace crossed her arms and frowned. "Isn't it bad luck to see the bride on her wedding day? Anarchy, why are you here?"

"Max lost his mind last night." I glanced at the kitchen clock. "This morning. I called Anarchy."

She rubbed her hand across her forehead. "I didn't hear anything."

"Sweetie, you could sleep through Armageddon."

She scowled. "Was there anyone here?"

"No," I replied immediately.

Anarchy frowned. "I didn't see anyone." He scratched behind Max's ears. "But this guy is never wrong."

"Who?" Grace demanded. "Who was it?"

Anarchy's expression darkened. "Your mom found three bodies this week."

"Do you think she's in danger?"

"We'll be on a plane for Italy tomorrow and when we get back, I promise I'll keep her safe."

"What about Grace?" A sick feeling swirled in my stomach.

"What about me?"

"I can't leave if someone is sneaking around the house at night."

"Sure you can."

"No. I can't. I'm not stepping foot out of Kansas City till I know you'll be safe while I'm gone."

Grace rolled her eyes.

I remained resolute.

She crossed her arms and tried a second eyeroll.

I wanted a trip to Italy with my new husband more than I'd ever wanted anything. But I wasn't hopping a flight if Grace might be in danger. I mirrored her crossed arms.

"Fine," she huffed. "Then we'd better figure out who the killer is, because your flight leaves at eleven tomorrow morning." She settled on a stool at the kitchen island. "What do we know?"

Anarchy's lips quirked.

"Honey, this is a police matter."

"Nope." She glared at me as if I were particularly slow this morning. "If it means you miss your honeymoon, it's a family matter."

Our staring match was long and stubborn and a complete draw.

"It won't hurt to talk it out, Ellison."

"Traitor." The softness in my voice told him I didn't mean it.

"Come on," Grace whined. "Please."

"Fine," I ceded.

Grace jumped up from her stool and paced like Perry Mason. "Tell me what happened that afternoon at the thrift shop."

"I need more coffee."

"Hurry up." Grace was as pushy as Mother.

When my cup was full, I sat on a stool next to Anarchy. "I dropped off some items late on Wednesday afternoon, then came home for a second load. At some point during my trip home, someone killed Avery Stallard and the shop manager, Rose."

Grace clasped her hands behind her back and kept pacing.

"Avery Stallard." She stopped and stared at us. "Who had a motive?"

Slightly disconcerted that my daughter had morphed into a TV detective, I replied, "Her husband, her stepchildren, and possibly the man with whom she had an affair."

"What about the shop manager? Did anyone want her dead?"

"We haven't found a motive," Anarchy replied. "There's no money for heirs. And while she wasn't beloved, she didn't have enemies that we can find."

"Her job was her life." I took a bracing sip of coffee. "She didn't want to retire."

"Then why was she?" asked Grace.

"A handful of members thought it was time for new, younger blood."

"Would they kill to get rid of her?"

"No." My answer was immediate. "Rose let her feelings be known, but if the committee decided she should retire, she'd retire."

Grace resumed her pacing. "So. Avery Stallard. Why would her husband want her dead? The affair?"

"Maybe. I also heard she tried getting pregnant with another man's baby."

Grace stopped her pacing and stared at me. The shock on her face was almost comical.

"She did that?"

"It appears so," Anarchy replied. "Peters is tracking down the man."

"Wow. So Mr. Stallard is a suspect. Does he have an alibi?"

"Not one we can corroborate. None of the Stallards do."

I stared into my coffee. "I talked to Dot last night."

"When?" Anarchy asked.

"Just before dinner, after I talked to Chef in the kitchen. I saw her in the ladies' lounge, and she asked me to tell you why she and Tori were at the thrift shop. Also, she says she and Tori are innocent."

"Hold the phone." Grace waved a finger my way. "They were both at the thrift shop the day of the murder?"

They were both at the thrift shop, or at least in the parking lot, during the murder. "They had a deal with Rose to buy their mother's things."

"Why would they need to do that?"

"Because Avery gave them to the shop rather than letting the kids take them."

"Seems like a motive for murder. They're definitely suspects." She walked to the back door and peered into the yard. "What about the woman who drowned?"

"We're still waiting on the medical examiner's report," Anarchy replied.

"Mom, you don't know anything. Why would someone creep around the house?" She paced the length of the kitchen, wheeled, and stared at Anarchy and me as if we were deliberately withholding clues. "We must be missing something."

Brnng, brnng.

We all turned toward the phone.

"It's not yet eight," said Grace.

"Maybe it's about a delivery." I picked up the receiver. "Hello."

"Ellison."

"Good morning, Mother."

"You're angry with me."

"I'm not happy."

"I don't blame you. I'm calling to apologize."

"You are?"

"I'm sorry I drank too much, sorry I disrupted your rehearsal, and sorry I missed the dinner."

"I wish you'd been there."

"Yes. Harrington told me your future sister-in-law sang."

"'Alone Again.'"

"Isn't that about getting jilted at the altar?"

"It is. She added extra verses."

"Your father said Oscar's toast was memorable."

I glanced at Anarchy. "I'll never forget it."

"Something about fleeting happiness?"

I nodded, then remembered she couldn't see me. "That's right. And death."

"But the brother's wasn't bad?"

"River gave a nice toast."

Anarchy snorted. His brother had referenced Anarchy's job, my propensity for finding bodies, and the likelihood our marriage would be murder.

"Your father said Marjorie spoke."

"She did." A rambling speech which mentioned being my real sister six times. "We could have used you there." Mother would have cut Marjorie off after the first five minutes.

"What time should I arrive today?"

"The wedding's at seven thirty, Mother. How about a quarter after?"

"I can come early."

The last thing I needed was a hungover Frances Walford chasing away the caterer or florist. "We have everything covered. We'll see you this evening."

She replied with silence.

"Thanks for calling, Mother."

"You know I love you."

"I know. I love you, too."

"I want what's best for you."

"Anarchy is best for me."

"You're sure?"

"Positive."

"Fine. I won't say another word."

Neither of us believed that. "Mother, I have a million things to do." I didn't. "I'll see you tonight."

She sighed. "Fine."

"Goodbye." I eased the receiver into the cradle.

"Are we still going out for breakfast?" asked Grace.

"Yes," Anarchy replied.

"But we haven't solved the murder."

"We can discuss it over pancakes."

Grace nodded at Anarchy's phenomenal idea. "I'll go change."

She raced up the stairs, and Anarchy pulled me into his arms. "Less than twelve hours till you're my wife."

I smiled up at him. "I have something for you."

He frowned.

"I planned to give it to you tonight, but you seem fixated on the time. I'll be right back." I pulled loose of his hold and headed to the foyer, where I'd stashed his gift in the bombé chest.

With the wrapped package in my hands, I hurried back to the kitchen.

Anarchy's gaze shifted to the gift. "What's that?"

"A wedding present." I held it out. "Open it."

"You didn't need to do this."

"Yes, I did. I wanted you to have something special to mark the day."

He slipped off the bow, ripped the paper, and opened the box.

"Read the inscription."

He turned the watch in his hands and read. His mouth thinned and his shoulders stiffened.

"You don't like it?" He didn't look happy.

He ran a finger over the inscription, then slipped the watch on his wrist. "This is the best gift I've ever received." He pulled me back into his arms and kissed me. Deeply.

Grace's Dr. Scholl's clattering on the back steps finally drove us apart.

She burst into the kitchen, took in my swollen lips and mussed hair, and offered us an epic eyeroll. "You guys, I'm hungry. Go get ready." She glanced at the clock. "You have ten minutes."

"Someone wants pancakes."

She grinned. "That and we have a murder to solve."

CHAPTER TWELVE

Saturday morning pancakes, at least when those pancakes were blueberry and served with an ewer of syrup, distracted Grace from solving murders.

Together, the three of us—Anarchy, Grace, and I—sat at a table at Putsch's Coffee House and sipped coffee. Well, Anarchy and I sipped coffee. Grace drank orange juice. Looking around our little table made my vision shimmer, and I clutched my coffee cup in gratitude for this little family. My family. Tonight, Anarchy and I would make it official.

Grace poured more syrup on her pancakes. My daughter was slender as a reed, but she usually counted calories. Obviously not today.

I looked at my plate filled with scrambled eggs and dry toast and decided I was too nervous to eat. I stuck a spoon in my coffee, stirred, sipped, and sighed.

"Your relationship with coffee isn't healthy." Grace spoke around a mouthful of syrup-laden pancake.

"My relationships aren't healthy without coffee," I replied. Dealing with Mother required caffeine. Same with Libba.

Frankly, Grace was no prize first thing in the morning on a school day.

"Is that why you talk to Mr. Coffee?" She gave me a cheeky grin.

"Among other reasons." Mr. Coffee was also cheerful, dependable, and generous.

"You realize he can't talk back?"

"Neither can Max, but I talk to him too." Mr. Coffee and Max did talk back. That Grace didn't hear them was not my fault.

Anarchy watched our exchange with a satisfied smile.

Grace halted a pancake-heavy fork halfway to her mouth. "We still need to solve the murders."

"Or you can stay with your grandparents while we're gone."

She dropped her fork into a pool of syrup. "Aggie will be at our house. No way am I staying with Granna."

"Granna doesn't get prowlers." The prowlers wouldn't dare.

"Granna doesn't find bodies."

"My point exactly."

"So I suffer because you find bodies?" Grace abandoned her pancakes and held out her hands to Anarchy in appeal. "Tell Mom she's crazy."

"She wants to keep you safe," Anarchy replied.

We were a united front. If Grace had begged for my late husband's aid in undercutting my authority, he'd have loaned her a machete. I reached under the table and gave Anarchy's hand a grateful squeeze.

"Nope. Let's figure this out." Grace's gaze caught on something over my shoulder. Her face registered annoyance, then she slapped on a pleasant smile, rose to her feet, and extended her hand. "Good morning, Mr. and Mrs. Gilchrist."

Anarchy stood and nodded good morning.

Laura took Grace's hand. "Nice to see you, Grace. You look lovely. Ellison, she has such nice manners."

I nodded my approval. "We try."

Anarchy and Charles shook hands.

Laura's curious gaze scanned our full table. "I didn't expect to see you out and about today."

"I'm assured I'll only be in the way at home."

A frown creased her brow. "Isn't it bad luck to see the bride on her wedding day?"

Anarchy grinned. "Worth the risk."

Charles chuckled. "Spoken like a man in love. We wish you every happiness, and we'll let you get back to your breakfast." He took his wife's elbow and steered her toward the door.

The Gilchrists moved on, and Anarchy and Grace resumed their seats.

Grace's eyes followed the couple until they exited the restaurant. "She's nice."

"She is," I agreed.

"Are they happy?" she asked. It was an unusual question from a teenager.

I stared at her. "What do you mean?"

She studied her pancakes and poked at a blueberry. Her cheeks flushed.

"What have you heard?"

"Nothing specific." Grace chased the blueberry around the rim of her plate. "Piper came home early from field hockey practice and Mr. Gilchrist was at her house." Piper was one of Grace's many friends.

"Aren't Charles and Piper's father friends?"

"That's what Piper's mom said. She told Piper he was dropping off a tool he'd borrowed. But Piper thought the vibe was weird."

"Piper enjoys drama." This was the girl who had hysterics over broken nails, went on a starvation diet when she gained a pound, and cried a three-week river when the boy who'd asked her out twice switched his attention to another girl.

Grace couldn't argue my point, so she nodded and heaped the blueberry and an enormous bite of pancake onto her fork. "You're right." She chewed, then washed the pancake down with orange juice. "What are the Stallards' alibis?"

And we were back to murder.

"They don't hold up," said Anarchy.

"So any of the Stallards could have committed murder?"

Anarchy nodded, and I checked the tables near us. The last thing I needed was for anyone to overhear this conversation.

Satisfied that the older ladies at the nearest table (both of whom wore hats and smart suits and probably had their gloves folded neatly in their purses) were not paying the slightest attention to us, I said, "Grace, keep your voice down."

She rolled her eyes.

"I mean it. Tori and Dot are dear friends. We will not gossip about them in public."

"But in private it's okay?" So much sass.

I leaned forward, lowered my voice, and used a tone from Mother's bag of tricks. "They are legitimate suspects in a murder investigation, but that does not need to be broadcast to every table at Putsch's."

Her juice glass met the table with too much force. "We need to solve this. You are not canceling your honeymoon, and I am not spending two weeks at Granna's." Perhaps sensing she'd pushed I-am-teenager-hear-me-roar too far, she softened her tone. "Please, Mom. Don't make me."

When I didn't reply, she added, "We have the rest of the day to figure this out."

"Ellison?"

Again? There were more table hoppers at Putsch's on a Saturday morning than at the club on prime rib night. I turned in my chair and dredged up a smile. "Carrie, how nice to see you."

Grace and Anarchy stood.

"Please meet my daughter, Grace, and my fiancé, Anarchy Jones. This is Carrie Hilliard."

Carrie was a decade younger than me. She was pretty and bubbly and hip. She smiled brightly and waved rather than shaking hands. "Nice to meet you."

"Likewise," Anarchy replied. "How do you know Ellison?"

Carrie blinked and tapped her lips. "The League!" She sounded pleased and surprised she'd found the answer. "We've worked on committees together."

"I haven't seen you in ages. What's your assignment this year?" Each year, League members had volunteer assignments. Some were hands-on—helping disadvantaged children learn to read, working in soup kitchens, or staffing the thrift shop. Others were more managerial—marketing the League's cookbook, handling the organization's financials, or managing its fundraisers.

Carrie offered me a dazzling smile. "Thrift-shop management."

She was one of the women set on retiring Rose? I scowled. Deeply.

Carrie looked at my face, and her smile faded into a deep frown. "I'm so sorry. I forgot. You found Rose and Avery Stallard. How awful for you."

The horrific crime scene flashed against my eyelids, but it wasn't the reason for my scowl.

"Poor Rose." Carrie shook her head sadly. "We were lucky to have her."

"So you're not one of the members who was forcing her into retirement?" I shouldn't have said it, but I still carried the stinging weight of Rose's family's anger. Also, forcing a long-term employee into poverty was despicable.

Carrie flushed. "You heard about that?"

"I visited with Rose's family. They're bitter."

Her flush deepened to a brick red. "When did you last volunteer at the thrift shop?"

"It's been a while," I admitted.

Carrie's lips flattened. "We had complaints from provisionals. Rose had them waxing the racks."

Grace's forehead wrinkled. "What does that mean?"

"Rose made the provisionals wipe the rod part of the racks with wax paper. She said the hangers slid easier when the pole was waxed."

"Did they?" Anarchy's lips were pinched as if he were trying not to laugh. "Also, what's a provisional?"

"A provisional member," I explained. "They have to complete a certain number of volunteer hours and classes before they're offered full membership." I turned my attention to Carrie. "A handful complain each year."

"This was more than a handful. They claimed Rose created work." Carrie's voice lacked inflection, as if she'd said those exact words many times before. "Those volunteer hours could have been used elsewhere doing something productive. Also, she got rid of pricers' preference."

"She did? When?" Pricers' preference was a major perk. If a League member volunteered to price donations and found something she wanted, say a cashmere sweater, she could price the sweater according to the shop's guidelines, and buy it before it went to the sales floor.

High-end merchandise seldom made it out of the back room.

And I knew for a fact that A-quality dresses and suits (St. John, Halston, even Chanel) were frequently priced as B-quality merchandise. It wasn't as if the extra ten dollars made a difference to the women buying the clothes, but everyone loved a bargain. The same thing happened with men's clothes. I'd witnessed Joanie Higgins and Betsy Graden an in all-out catfight over a Burberry trench. Hair was pulled. Nails were unsheathed. Strongly worded letters about appropriate behavior for members were sent.

Despite Joanie and Betsy's epic brawl, pricers' preference was popular with the volunteers. The hope of finding a Gucci bag or Ferragamo pumps made opening boxes and bags of other people's old clothes bearable.

"I can't tell you exactly when, but it's been in the past few months." Carrie crossed her arms. "It's high time the thrift shop moved into the seventies."

"My understanding is that Rose asked to stay on until she could depend on her annuities."

Carrie shook her head. "We need that shop to make money. And lately, revenues are down. It was time for a change." She grimaced as if she'd finally heard what she was saying—that an organization dedicated to helping people put profits ahead of a long-term staff member's well-being. "It's tragic what happened to her, but now we can make some changes."

I was wrong; she'd obviously missed the putting-profits-over-people part of her remarks.

Anarchy and Grace still stood. Their polite faces had morphed into brittle masks. Carrie waved at them. "I'm keeping you from your breakfast. Please sit."

Neither Grace nor Anarchy moved a muscle.

Carrie took a step back (maybe she'd finally realized something was amiss). "I won't keep you. Nice to see you, Ellison. And nice to meet you." She nodded at my fiancé and daughter. "Ciao."

Grace narrowed her eyes and watched Carrie return to her table. "I don't think I'll join the League."

"Don't let your grandmother hear you say that." Mother would have a conniption fit. "The League makes a tremendous positive difference in the community."

That earned me an eyeroll.

"Eat your pancakes."

WHEN WE RETURNED HOME, the driveway was full of trucks. Grace and I climbed out of Anarchy's car, but rather than climbing the front steps with me, she circled the sedan and slipped into the passenger's seat.

"Where are you going?"

"We have an errand." She gave me an airy wave. "I'll be back in an hour."

"Might be a little longer," said Anarchy.

"You heard him."

I frowned, and Anarchy got out of the car long enough to give me a quick kiss goodbye.

"See you soon."

"Where are you going?"

"It's a surprise." He kissed my forehead.

"Don't be so nosy," said Grace through the open car window.

"Fine." I watched them drive away, then stepped into a house crawling with people, all of whom looked at me as if I were in the way.

I peeked into the kitchen. "Good morning."

Aggie wore a lime-green kaftan covered with daisies. Her orange hair stood out from her head at odd angles, and rather than offering a welcoming smile, she narrowed harried eyes.

"What are you doing right now?"

I held up innocent hands. "Nothing."

"Would you please take Max for a run?" Her enormous lime-green hoop earrings jiggled with unexpressed ire. "He's made it his mission to be underfoot."

A crash came from the family room.

I jumped.

Aggie winced.

An unidentified man swore a blue streak.

Rather than deal with the problem in the family room, I

headed for the stairs. "I'll change right away." I hurried up the back steps, threw on shorts and a t-shirt, jammed my feet into running shoes, and returned to the kitchen in record time.

Aggie handed me Max's leash. "Thank you. You're the only one here without a job today."

I folded its leather length into three neat loops. "Where is he?"

"A florist's assistant chased him out of the family room. Try the backyard."

I stepped outside, where a small army of workers finished transforming my patio into a romantic oasis. "Sorry to interrupt." Six heads turned my direction. "Have you seen a gray dog?"

Six expressions soured.

"In the house," said a young woman who held up her long hair with two sticks and a bit of embossed leather.

The leash in my hand did nothing to earn their forgiveness. I escaped their hard eyes, cut through the kitchen pretending I didn't notice the unhappy purse of Aggie's lips, and stopped in the front hall. "Max?"

"Oh. My. God."

I followed the strange near-hysterical voice to the dining room, where a ravaged palm tree and a half-ton of potting soil covered the floor.

A man wearing a lavender t-shirt and bellbottom jeans pressed his hands to his cheeks. He squinted, slowly surveyed the wreckage, then rubbed his eyes. "Dude."

Rather than gaping at the floor, the man should have focused on the dog. Max had obviously been after something in the basket that held the tree. My dog's head now protruded from the bottom of the basket while its wider portion circled his shoulders.

"What did you do?" I gasped. A stupid question. It was perfectly obvious Max had killed the palm. Equally obvious, he was deeply perturbed by the basket wrapped around his neck.

He shook his head wildly, spraying random bits of dirt and plant matter everywhere—the table, the walls, the man's lavender shirt. The basket didn't budge.

"Max!"

He froze and gave me a half-second of his attention. Long enough for me to notice the wild whites of his eyes. Then he took off running.

I chased. "Max!" My panicked dog ignored my call and ran through the kitchen. I heard the clanging crash of a sheet pan meeting the floor seconds before I passed through the door and saw Aggie's horrified expression.

There was no time to help her clean up. "Which way did he go?"

She pointed to the family room, and I followed.

Not fast enough.

Max ran smack into a young woman holding a full watering can—a large can meant for garden use. Why was it inside the house?

The woman teetered.

I held my breath.

She fell.

The watering can went up (completing two full rotations) before gravity did its job and the can met the floor.

Water exploded. It soaked the woman and the carpet. It splattered the furniture and me. It flooded the hardwood floors.

There were low, ugly murmurs.

Someone was going to kill my dog. I resisted the very real urge to back out of the room and let them. "I'm so sorry."

"Is this really your dog?" More of an accusation than a question from the sodden woman.

"He's not usually so troublesome."

"Troublesome?" She vibrated with an unnamed emotion.

"Ten Cent Beer Night at Cleveland Stadium was troublesome. The Cuban Missile crisis was troublesome. OPEC is troublesome. That beast is a disaster."

She wasn't saying anything I hadn't heard before. "Again, I'm so, so sorry." Maybe she'd hear the sincerity in the extra *so*. "Are you okay?"

"I'm fine," the woman bit out.

I shifted my gaze to my dog. "Max!"

Two of the florist's assistants had him cornered.

Max shook his head, hard. The basket remained wedged in place, but the last of the potting soil landed on the wet carpet and dissolved into muddy spots.

Aggie was going to kill him. Then me.

"Sit!"

My dog looked left. He looked right. He considered me with amber eyes, decided he was well and truly corralled, and, with a sigh, settled on his haunches.

I raced forward and fumbled under the basket until I found his collar. I gripped it tightly.

"You're coming with me."

I was tempted to pull the basket over his head, but what if I scratched his eyes? The last thing we needed was an emergency trip to the vet. Instead, I offered a weak apologetic wave to the angry workers in the family room and dragged Max into the kitchen, where Aggie scraped ruined canapés off the floor.

More than happy to clean the floor for her, Max strained against my hold.

I hated to interrupt her, hated to ask for a favor, but if I loosened my fingers, Max might run again. "Aggie, scissors?"

She rose from her knees and glared at Max as if she'd like to stab him. Multiple times. I held my breath until she put a pair of sharp kitchen shears in my hand.

"Hold still." I cut through the basket, clipped the leash onto his collar, and offered Aggie a tentative smile. "Should I still take him? If I go now, I'm leaving a huge mess."

"I don't care." Her gaze drifted to the counter where I'd put down the shears. The murderous gleam in her eyes was worrisome. "No one cares. We'll handle the mess. Just get him out of the house."

"Come on." I tugged at the leash. "Let's run until you drop." Given the trouble he'd already caused, maybe, for once, Max would tire before I did.

I crossed my fingers but did not hold my breath. Max possessed endless energy.

"You'll let Grace know where I am?"

"Just go."

I went.

CHAPTER THIRTEEN

Max and I walked to Loose Park with the late morning sun warm on our shoulders. Soon spring would give way to summer's humidity, but today was perfect.

Perfect if I didn't count the lynch mob I'd left at the house. "What were you thinking?"

Max trotted next to me, and his rear end wriggled with his emphatic tail wag. Almost as if he were pleased with all he'd accomplished.

The palm, the potting soil, Aggie's canapés, the geyser in the family room, and, given the level of ire when I arrived, some other equally devastating misdeeds. "Do you realize what a mess you made?"

He lifted his nose in the air and tugged on the leash. Messes were not a dog's problem. Messes were a human problem. Also, we'd arrived at the park, and he was eager to run.

As soon as my feet and Max's paws hit the pathway, we jogged.

For now, his pace matched mine, the very picture of an obedient dog. I wasn't fooled. Max might trot next to me, but he preferred hell-for-leather sprints that ended with a small animal in his jaws. He'd rip my arm out to chase a squirrel or rabbit.

One lap.

Two laps.

Three laps around the park. Sweat beaded my brow and ran between my breasts, and Max's tongue lolled from the side of his mouth.

Four laps.

"Shall we take a break?" I gasped. We'd run almost six miles, and I needed a rest.

He flashed me a mischievous doggy grin. Had I made even a dent in his energy supply? I'd decimated my own.

I slowed our pace to a walk. "Maybe you should spend the afternoon with Pansy."

Max made no objection.

"Let's sit." I collapsed onto a shady bench. Max flopped to the ground at my feet and eyed a squirrel who clung to an oak's trunk.

I closed my eyes and tried to slow my breath. Usually running cleared my head. Not today. I was too excited, too nervous. There was too much on my mind.

"You remember McCallister?" Anarchy's adopted cat posed a problem. He and Max had already had a disastrous encounter. An encounter that resulted in chaos as awful as Max's morning achievements. Fortunately, Peters was cat-sitting while we were in Italy. We had two weeks to figure out how a reckless feline and a canine determined to grab a cat by its tail could cohabitate without razing the house. "He's coming to live with us, and you need to dial back the destruction."

Max flashed me a dangerous doggy grin.

"Please." My tone cajoled, warned, threatened.

His grin broadened and his pink tongue made no promises.

I leaned back and breathed deep. McCallister and Max's rocky relationship was the least of my problems. Unsolved murders, a house covered in potting soil hours before our wedding, the wedding itself, and our families were far more pressing issues. But it was easier to focus on the small problem than the big ones. "Pretty please? With sugar?"

"You're talking to yourself?"

My shoulders tightened at the sound of Prudence Davies's voice.

Max growled.

"Where's Pansy?" she asked.

I turned my head and scowled at the woman who topped my list of least favorite people. She wore shorts, a t-shirt, and running shoes, but unlike me, she wasn't a sweaty mess. Her hair was perfect. And makeup improved her face. I was struck by the sudden certainty she'd come to the park in pursuit of a man. "Pansy lives with Charlie Ardmore."

Prudence gave Pansy, a gorgeous golden who made Max's destruction look like amateur hour, to me. I'd wisely given Pansy to Charlie. That he still spoke to me was a daily miracle.

A cat-that-swallowed-the canary smile curled her frosted pink lips. "I should visit."

"Charlie's not like Henry." A cheating barnacle on the hull of humanity. "Also, he's dating Libba." I winced. That was the wrong thing to say. Prudence regarded other women's claims on men as a personal challenge. How she attracted men was a mystery. Sugar and spice and everything nice had aged into vinegar and acid and everything evil. Also, Prudence had horse teeth. I'd spent too much time wondering how Prudence lured men (especially my husband) to her bed. There was only one possible explanation—her hoo-ha knew more magic tricks than Doug Henning.

She of the magic hoo-ha plopped onto the bench next to me, and my shoulders tightened until they brushed my earlobes.

"Relax. I don't want the dog."

"And Charlie?"

"I don't want him either." Which begged a disturbing question.

"What do you want?" She'd stopped to talk to me for a reason.

"A job."

I blinked. "A job?"

"That's what I just said."

"Doing what?" Destroying marriages? Pinch hitting for the devil? Teaching magic hoo-ha classes?

"A job at your bank."

It wasn't my bank. It was Grace's bank. "The bank?"

"This conversation will go much faster if you don't repeat every word I say."

"Does that mean it will end quicker?" I was on board with that.

I expected her to snarl. Maybe go for my throat. I shifted to the end of the bench and wondered if I had the energy to outrun her.

She laughed. Brayed, which was more in keeping with her horse-teeth persona.

I rubbed my sweaty face. "Why would you ask me for a job?"

"You have a bank."

Yes and no. Also, immaterial. "Why work for me? There have to be thousands of possible employers."

She glared at her hands in her lap. "Desperate times. Desperate measures."

"You hate me." And the feeling was mutual. "Also, don't you have a job?"

"I earn half what the men do and work twice as hard." I'd never heard her sound so bitter.

Unless she was talking about me.

"Why ask me?"

"Please."

A "please" from Prudence boggled the mind, but I remained steadfast. "No."

"Give me a good reason."

I had a million reasons. She'd slept with my late husband. She had fewer morals than a tomcat. She'd frighten the customers. "I can't think about this now. I'm getting married today."

"I hope you booked extra time at the salon. You'll need it." There was the Prudence I knew, the woman who insulted me with aplomb.

"I'm sorry. Weren't you just asking me for a job?"

She flushed. "Old habits. I apologize."

She apologized? Prudence never expressed remorse. I snuck a peek at the woman sitting next to me. Was it really Prudence? Had some otherworldly entity possessed her body? She watched a couple of kids toss a Frisbee and sat in silence, waiting for a good reason I wouldn't hire her.

I had no frame of reference for enemies asking for favors and no clue how to respond when they refused to listen. Not just no, but hell no.

She glanced at me and let the silence stretch.

I focused on the sound of laughing children enjoying their morning in the park, the gentle breeze ruffling the leaves, and the rasp of Max's breath. I had to. If I thought about Prudence, my head might explode.

"Why would I give you a job?"

"I'm a hard worker."

My brows rose. "No."

"You'll change your mind."

That was about as likely as Grace giving up the telephone line in her bedroom. "No."

Her eyes narrowed. "I know something."

About money? Banking? Economics? A shiver that had

nothing to do with the breeze tightened my neck. Was she trying to blackmail me with a secret about Henry? "Oh?"

She crossed her arms, stretched her legs, and leaned against the bench's back. "Do you want to solve a murder?"

I searched her smirking face and found nothing but attitude. She was certain I'd trade information for employment. Her bait was tempting. If Peters caught Avery and Rose's killer, Anarchy and I could leave for Italy without worry for Grace's safety.

Prudence's hook swayed seductively. I licked my lips. I clenched my hands. I stayed strong. "Whatever you know, you should tell the police."

She brayed again.

I hadn't meant to be funny. "What if the killer decides you're next?"

She pressed her hands to her heart (or where her heart would be if she had one). "It almost sounds as if you care."

"I don't want anyone else to die. Not even you."

"How admirable."

"Tell the police, Prudence."

"I don't think I will." She held out a hand and inspected her manicure. Was she lying? Did she know something real? Or was this a diabolical ploy to manipulate me?

I didn't have time for Prudence's games. I stood. "Let's go, Max."

"Wait."

I paused and looked down at her on the bench.

The smirk still flirted with her lips. "The job?"

How many times did I have to say no? I stared at her for long seconds. Until the smirk melted away and her shoulders slumped. Was that a shimmer in her eyes or the sunlight sifting through oak leaves?

"Please?"

I gave her one tiny inch. "What do you know?"

"Lilly Frasier didn't drown on her own."

Dammit. I sank onto the bench and endured the what-are-you-doing censure in Max's gaze. "The police aren't positive it was a murder."

"Oh, it was murder."

"How can you be so sure?"

"She told me..." Prudence fixed her gaze on a couple walking hand in hand.

"Told you what?"

"The job?"

I'd been a fool. This wasn't about finding Lilly's killer; it was about Prudence getting what she wanted. Not a job. There was no way in heaven or hell she wanted to work for me. I stood. "Detective Rogan is in charge of the case. I'm sure he'll be in touch."

I made it three steps toward home before her voice stopped me. "Ellison. Wait."

I took another step.

"She was blackmailing someone."

Now I stopped. Waited for more. When Prudence remained silent, I said, "Let's go, Max."

"Wait! I don't know who she blackmailed. If I did, I'd tell you."

"Blackmail doesn't mean she was murdered."

"The timing is suspect."

Max tugged, and I let him lead me a few feet away. I felt Prudence's gaze between my shoulder blades and tensed for a knife in my back.

"I don't believe in coincidences."

Neither did I. And if Prudence was telling the truth (there was a fifty-fifty chance she was lying through her horse teeth), Lilly's murder on the heels of Avery and Rose's was a huge coincidence. So huge it was unbelievable. They had to be related.

A squirrel chittered in an oak's branches, and a man wearing eye-searingly short shorts jogged by.

Max peered into the tree as if the strength of his gaze might convince the squirrel to wander close to us.

Prudence's gaze followed the man.

What did she know? I hated myself for even wondering. I clenched my jaw and ignored the questions jostling for the front of the line.

"The job?"

The answers to the questions weren't worth dealing with Prudence on a daily basis. "I don't trust you. I'm not hiring you to work at Grace's bank."

Prudence grimaced. "She's Henry's daughter. You think I'd deliberately hurt her?"

"If it meant hurting me? Yes."

She flushed an ugly red. "I can't change your mind?"

"No."

"Then we have nothing left to say." She rose from the bench and walked away. I watched her. There was something off about the set of her shoulders and the rhythm of her gait. Was she crying? Pity welled in my heart. Pity. For Prudence. She'd gut me if she knew.

Minutes later, I rang Charlie's doorbell and scowled at Max. "You'd better hope he says yes."

Max sat and wagged his stubby tail.

The front door opened, and Charlie stared at me with a slack jaw.

Dried sweat, a limp ponytail, and a clenched jaw (thank you, Prudence) weren't exactly what a bride hoped for on her wedding day. But I couldn't look so bad he was speechless. Could I?

"My God, what happened to you?" he asked.

Well, that was less than flattering. "Nothing." I forced a smile. "May Max spend the rest of the day with you and Pansy? Please? We're just back from a run." Which explained the sweat and the limp ponytail. "He'll probably sleep for a few hours." Maybe. Possibly. Okay, doubtfully.

"Of course."

Gratitude filled my heart, and I handed Max's leash to Charlie.

"He can stay till tomorrow."

My answering smile rose from my toes. "You're the best. Thank you."

"I'll see you tonight." Charlie's tone made it sound like I'd need every second to clean up. With one last bewildered glance, he led Max into his house.

I returned home, and Grace pounced the minute I walked through the door. "Where have you been?"

"I took Max for a run."

"Where is he?"

"Charlie's."

She wrinkled her nose. "You ran far."

"Are you saying I smell?"

"You might want to shower before Anarchy changes his mind."

"He's here?" I'd assumed he had other, better things to do.

She nodded.

"Where?"

"Helping Aggie move the wet rug out of the family room." She gave me a look unique to mothers and daughters. There was censure and love and judgment and the unwelcome realization that we reflected on each other. "Seriously, Mom. Go shower." Grace didn't want her reflection to stink.

"Fine." I hurried up the front steps, hit my bedroom, and peeled off my fragrant clothes.

In the shower, I soaped and shampooed and conditioned and shaved and lingered in the spray, framing my upcoming conversation with Anarchy.

So, I saw Prudence Davies...

About those murders...

There was a real possibility Prudence's revelation might derail my honeymoon.

Honey, there's something Peters should know...

The last of the conditioner rinsed from my hair, I turned off the water and wrapped myself in a fluffy towel.

Tap, tap.

"Who is it?"

"Me," said Anarchy. "We need to talk, and I don't have much time."

"Hold on." I wrapped my head in a towel.

"I'm needed at the hotel."

The hotel? I opened the door. "Is everything okay?"

"My sister has a crisis."

"Is she alright?"

"Journey has a crisis most days. Twice on Mondays."

"So not really a crisis. What do we need to talk about?"

He peered over my shoulder into the steamy bathroom and bit his lower lip.

"Is something wrong?"

"No! No. I was going to give this to you later, but Journey might claim the rest of my afternoon. I hope—" he held out a ring box "—I hope you like it."

I opened the box and stared.

"The stone belonged to my grandmother. She called it Big Blue."

"I see why." The ring in the box was set with a sapphire the size of my thumbnail.

"Something blue for the wedding."

I was speechless.

"Something old, something new, something borrowed, something blue." He held out a coin. "This is the sixpence for your shoe. I figured you'd have the rest covered."

I rose up on my toes and wrapped my arms around his neck. "Thank you."

"Wait." He pulled away from me. "Let's try it on." He slipped the sapphire onto the ring finger of my right hand. "Does it fit?"

I held out my hand and admired the sparkle. "Perfectly. Thank you."

"I'll take that kiss now."

We didn't speak for long moments.

When he pulled away a second time, I said, "I need to tell you something before you go." I recounted my conversation with Prudence.

Anarchy frowned and rubbed his chin. "I'll let Peters and Rogan know."

"That's it?"

His brows rose. "What do you mean?"

"I worried you might postpone our honeymoon."

He wrapped his arms around me and stared at me with the most gorgeous eyes on the planet. "Nothing, and I do mean nothing, will stop me from making you my wife and taking you to Italy."

It was as if he were tempting fate.

CHAPTER FOURTEEN

Thirty minutes later, with dry hair, makeup, and clothes that didn't smell like a locker room, I descended the front stairs.

Mother met me in the front hall. "I'm here to apologize in person."

Where had she come from? Why hadn't Grace or Aggie warned me? Mother, here to apologize? What next? The apocalypse? My hand gripped the newel post, and I waited for more.

She stared at me as if it were my turn to speak.

"Was that your apology?"

She lifted her nose. "There's no call to be difficult."

"You got so sloshed at my wedding rehearsal that you missed the dinner, and you can't say the words, 'I'm sorry'?"

"At least I came to the rehearsal."

"When I was a kid, you taught me one bad act does not excuse another." I pretended not to see her wince. "You're not forgiven."

Mother frowned at me and tilted her head to the side, as if I'd suddenly started speaking a foreign language.

That's when I knew. "Daddy sent you. He made you apologize. You don't feel one iota of remorse."

"Please, lower your voice." Her eyes narrowed. "Is that how you're wearing your hair?" Avoidance. A classic Mother technique.

Two could play the avoidance game. "If you'll excuse me—" I turned my back on her "—I have things to do." I didn't.

"What things?"

"Things."

Mother grabbed my wrist and forced me to face her. "What's that?" Her gaze fixed on my hand.

Big Blue had caught her eye. "My wedding gift from Anarchy." No one, not even Mother, could find fault with the ring.

"It's a bit flashy, don't you think?" And she proved me wrong.

"No. I think it's absolutely beautiful." I spoke through gritted teeth. "The stone belonged to his grandmother."

"He didn't buy you a gift?"

"He had the stone reset. Tell your friends it's a family heirloom." Incontrovertible fact: jewels became more covetable when they'd been in the family for generations.

"Well, if you like it..."

No one, not one single soul, would blame me if I slapped her. "As apologies go, this one is especially bad."

She sniffed.

"You didn't apologize and now you've insulted the very lovely gift from my future husband."

Mother rubbed a circle on the center of her forehead. "It's only because I want what's best for you."

"If you plan on saying one word against Anarchy, you can leave now."

Mother's sharp intake of breath was the only hint I'd surprised her. Or displeased her. Tomato, tomahto. "Just you wait." She sounded almost heartbroken (I wasn't fooled).

"Someday you'll watch Grace make a mistake, and you'll remember this moment."

"I hope I learn from your mistakes."

She exhaled. "I can't talk to you anymore."

She couldn't bulldoze me anymore.

"I want you to be happy."

"Anarchy makes me happy."

She rolled her eyes, then covered the upper half of her face with her hand. "Geoffrey Stallard called your father this morning and asked us to dinner."

I blinked at the change in subject. But that was one of the attributes that made Mother dangerous. She zigged when I expected her to zag.

"Did he kill his wife?"

I stared at her.

"Well? Did he? We distanced ourselves when he married that woman. I don't want to renew the friendship if he's going away for murder."

I took a deep, calming breath and reminded myself that Mother and Daddy's relationship with Geoffrey Stallard was not my problem. "What did Daddy say?"

"Your father." She shook her head. "Of course he accepted. Without consulting me." Poor Daddy had made a major misstep. Mother handled the social calendar. "Then we realized Geoffrey meant tonight. Apparently, he didn't realize you're getting married this evening."

"It's not as if he's invited." Also, he'd had rather a lot on his plate.

"We had a valid reason to cancel. But the next time he calls?"

"He's one of Daddy's oldest friends."

"That doesn't mean he's innocent."

Did Geoffrey kill Avery and Rose? Did Lilly find out? Or had she discovered the truth about someone else? How were the murders connected? I glanced at my watch. I was getting married in less than seven hours, but murder kept poking its nose in my day. Maybe I was selfish, but I wanted a murder-free wedding day. Avery and Rose and Lilly's lives were over, but I felt like mine was finally beginning, and I wanted today, and the next two weeks, to celebrate.

"Am I keeping you?" Mother's tone was arctic.

"Things to do." Like see if there was lunch in the kitchen.

"About Geoffrey?"

"I don't know, Mother."

"Was it one of his children? Because raising a murderer reflects poorly on the parents. Are you sure your friends aren't killers?"

I'd been holding on to *passably pleasant* by my fingernails. I lost my hold. "I don't know," I snapped.

Mother flinched. "Please, lower your voice."

She was hungover. There was no other explanation. Rather than offer aspirin or ice water, I raised my voice. "Tori and Dot were buying their mother's things from the thrift shop because Avery chose to be vindictive."

"That reminds me." She'd zagged again.

"Of?"

"Rose called earlier this week. I left some papers in a handbag I donated. I need to swing by and pick them up."

"Papers?"

"Something to do with the car registration."

"You had registration papers?" Mother might manage the calendar, but Daddy handled all things even vaguely official.

"Your father asked me to put them in a safe place."

"So you gave them to the thrift shop?"

She scowled at me. "It was an accident. I can't be the first woman who's donated without first checking pockets or going through the zippered parts of a purse."

She was right about that.

Mother lifted a finger and pointed at me. "Actually, it's your fault."

I had the greatest respect for the pointy end of Mother's fingernails. I retreated a step. "My fault?"

"If I wasn't so upset about your wedding, I would have remembered."

I simply stared. Sometimes there were no words.

"The shop is still closed." Mother sighed as if the two dead women were a personal inconvenience. "What about Paige? Did she kill Avery?"

"Avery held up Paige's trust distribution."

"Sounds like a motive. And James?"

"I have a sneaking suspicion James was there first."

"What do you mean?"

"James dated Avery first. It can't feel good when your dad steals your girl."

Mother's face scrunched as if she'd smelled three-day-old fish. "They all have motives."

"Especially Geoffrey. The woman tried to get pregnant with another man's baby and pass it off as his."

"Was she pregnant when she died?"

"If she was, Anarchy hasn't told me."

"Geoffrey didn't steal her from James." Mother glared at the light shining through the transom above the front door, and outside, a few birds fell from the sky. "That woman—that woman seduced him. Ensnared him. She—" Mother's distaste was writ clear on her face "—she became a sick obsession."

So Prudence wasn't the only woman with a magic hoo-ha. James probably resented losing Avery to his father.

"I'm not gossiping about the Stallards." Well, not any more than I already had. I headed toward the kitchen.

"Wait." Mother had more thoughts about my marriage. I sensed them hovering around her head.

I countered with a question. "Have you heard anything about

Lilly Frasier and her husband being proposed for club membership?"

Mother guffawed. "Heavens, no." Then she frowned. "Isn't she dead?" She pointed that accusing finger my way a second time. "You found her."

"She drowned."

"Then she can't join the club." There was triumph in Mother's tone. "Not that she ever had a hope of slipping past the membership committee."

I agreed with her about the membership committee. Not that I'd admit such. "Lilly drowned," I repeated. Surely that earned her a kind word.

"Don't pretend you liked her."

"I barely knew her. She died a horrible death."

"I heard there was more vodka than blood in her veins. She didn't feel a thing."

"Where did you hear that?"

"About the vodka?"

"Yes."

Mother frowned. "I'm not sure."

"Try to remember."

She glared at me. "Fine. But we need to talk about—"

Before we could return to the subject of my marriage, I asked, "What's up with Prudence Davies?"

"That awful woman? Why do you ask?"

"I saw her this morning. She asked for a job at the bank."

"I hope you turned her down."

"I did, but I wonder why she'd ask."

"Last I heard, she'd moved in with her mother. She may need to earn a living."

"But why ask me?"

"Excellent point." Mother stroked her chin. "Maybe she's planning an elaborate heist." The way Mother's mind worked was truly terrifying.

"She's not a criminal mastermind."

"Keep your friends close, but your enemies closer?" Truly, truly terrifying.

"Possibly. It just seemed odd."

"I'll never understand what Henry saw in that woman."

Again, I kept my magic hoo-ha theory to myself. Instead, I strode into the kitchen.

A tray of sandwiches, a bowl of fruit salad, and open bags of chips (both potato and corn) sat on the kitchen island.

I grabbed a paper plate and helped myself.

"Where's Aggie?"

"Around."

"What's all this?" She waved at the food, the paper plates and napkins, and the plastic forks.

"We have ten thousand workers here today. Aggie fed them." I set my plate on the counter and poured a glass of iced tea. "Please, help yourself."

Mother sniffed. Because I didn't serve her? Because I offered her the same lunch Aggie made for the help? Because she could? "I'm not hungry."

She did look a tad green.

"Maybe some iced tea?"

"Please."

I poured a second glass, handed it to her, and carried my plate and iced tea into the butler's pantry, a pass-through between the kitchen and the dining room large enough for a small table in front of a sunny window.

Mother sank into the closest chair, and I sat across from her and picked up my sandwich. "We're not discussing the wedding."

"Fine."

"Or my new in-laws."

"Are you sure?" Mother's smile was undiluted evil. "I heard Journey made quite an impression at the club."

"You're the one who insisted on having the rehearsal dinner there." I took a bite of ham and swiss and chewed with vigor.

"Where else?"

I covered my lips with my fingers and spoke around the sandwich in my mouth. "Stroud's."

"I'm sure your vegan soon-to-be sister-in-law would have loved a restaurant whose slogan is 'we choke our own chickens.'"

I imagined Journey in the Stroud's kitchen, laughed, and choked on a bit of ham.

When I stopped hacking and my eyes stopped watering, Mother reached across the table and patted my hand. "I want what's best for you."

"Then have enough faith to believe I know what best is." Best was Anarchy. And me. Married. Other than Grace, our families didn't matter. They wouldn't be living with us. Ever. Ever. Where was the salt? I needed a pinch to toss over my left shoulder. Instead, I crossed my fingers under the table.

"I'm sorry I ruined your rehearsal. I didn't do it on purpose." Her apology felt real.

"You didn't ruin anything. And I missed you at the dinner."

"You did?"

"I needed moral support."

"That woman?" She meant Celeste.

"And her husband."

"They're not our kind, dear." Just when Mother seemed human, she said things like that.

"I'm marrying their son."

"But you haven't. Not yet. You—"

"Maybe you should find a new way to look at things."

She tilted her head and a crease formed between her brows. "How so?"

"You see Anarchy as a homicide detective with questionable taste in sports coats."

"You admit they're questionable?"

"I'm in love, not blind. I see Anarchy differently. He's a brilliant, honorable man who makes my heart sing."

"And?"

"Two sides of the same man. You just need to look at him another way."

"I'll try."

This victory was too easy. I didn't trust it.

Mother reached across the table and stole a chip from my plate. "What's the father like?"

"Nothing like Anarchy. Oscar Jones hated me on sight."

"Then he's an idiot."

Brnng, brnng.

"Russell residence." Aggie's harried voice carried from the kitchen. "May I ask who's calling, please?" She listened. "One moment please."

A few seconds later, she stuck her head into the butler's pantry. "Bruce Alexander is on the phone."

I frowned. "Bruce? Really?"

"What does he want?" Mother demanded.

"One way to find out." I stood, walked to the kitchen, and picked up the receiver from the counter where Aggie, who'd already returned to another chore, had left it. "Hello."

"Ellison?"

"Bruce. How nice to hear from you."

"Sorry to bother you on your special day, but Carl Brown called me."

"Who?"

"Carl Brown, the bank manager."

"Ah." Now Bruce's call made sense. He sat on the bank's board. "What did Mr. Brown say?"

"He tells me you instructed him to give the female employees equal pay."

"Yes."

"I'm not sure you realize what you've done." But he was sure to tell me.

"I told Mr. Brown equal pay for equal work."

"Why would you do that?"

"Because it's fair."

"The bank can't afford it."

"Well, I'm set on equal pay, so if we can't pay the women more, we'll just have to cut the men's salaries."

Bruce answered with strangled silence.

Mother, who'd followed me into the kitchen, raised her brows.

I covered the receiver's mouthpiece. "It's unacceptable that the bank pays young women so little that they have to buy clothes at the thrift shop."

Mother's shoulders stiffened. "I should say so. Being parsimonious reflects poorly on you and Grace."

"We can't cut their pay." Bruce had reclaimed his voice. It boomed through the receiver.

"Then we'll live with a smaller profit. We are not paying women less."

"Ellison, be reasonable."

That was his response? Be reasonable?

"Bruce, I'm the board chairman. Grace owns eighty percent of the stock. If I say equal pay, there will be equal pay."

Mother nodded as if she approved. I raised a brow at her.

"Ellison, I realize you're emotional right now. You girls go a bit crazy when it comes to weddings." Condescension dripped from Bruce's voice. "Perhaps now isn't the time to make this decision."

I squeezed my eyes shut and tamped down the urge to scream. "This has nothing to do with emotion."

"Now, Ellison. You're new to this. You don't understand how business works."

"I believe I do."

"The girls get raises every year."

"Percentage raises."

"Yes."

"Bruce, if we give five percent raises, and women make two dollars an hour and men make three dollars an hour, men get a fifty percent bigger raise."

"That's one way to look at it. The other way is that everyone gets the same."

My free hand clenched tight enough that my nails cut half-moons into my skin. "Your way means less in the female employees' pockets."

"Ellison..."

"Equal pay, Bruce. That's final."

"But—"

"No buts. Now, if you'll excuse me, I have a million things to do." The only thing I had to do before the wedding was touch up my makeup and change my dress. "I expect equal pay by the time I return. We'll catch up in a few weeks." I hung up.

Mother pursed her lips. "That man is a weasel. I never understood why Henry put him on the board."

"Because he did anything Henry asked."

"It's nice that you want to offer the girls equal pay."

"They're women. And they deserve it."

She leaned against the door frame. "You've opened a can of worms. Can't the girls—women—find husbands? Then they wouldn't have to worry."

"Not all women want husbands. Not all women who want a husband find one. And not all husbands are good providers."

Mother held out her hand and studied her manicure. Closely. If she met my gaze, she'd have to admit I was right.

"In this world, a woman should be able to take care of herself."

"Yet you insist on getting married."

A growl rumbled in my chest. "I'm marrying Anarchy because I love him, not because I want him to pay my bills."

"You make it sound so mercenary."

"Mother, it's my wedding day. Let's not argue."

"I'm not the one arguing."

No one, not one single soul, would blame me if I murdered her.

CHAPTER FIFTEEN

The young man in the lavender shirt walked into the kitchen carrying a large plastic bucket. He blanched when he saw me. "The dog?"

"Max is spending the rest of the day next door."

"Groovy." He offered up a relieved smile, put the bucket in the sink, and turned on the tap. "Thank you for lunch, Mrs. Russell. That was really cool."

"You're welcome, but thank Aggie. She did all the work."

He nodded. Vaguely.

As the bucket filled, Mother beckoned to me from the doorway to the butler's pantry. "That young man smells funny," she whispered.

"He does," I agreed.

"I think he's high on marijuana." Her whisper had turned into a whisper-yell.

I glanced toward the sink. The man's back had stiffened.

"No one told him I'm marrying a cop." I spoke at full voice.

The man turned off the tap, grabbed his bucket, and disappeared faster than Mario Andretti on a final lap.

"He smoked marijuana in your house!"

"More likely, he snuck out to his car or truck."

Her eyes narrowed. "Well! It's inexcusable. Tell his boss. Report him to Anarchy. Call someone!"

"Mother."

"What?"

"Not today."

She opened her mouth, and I prepared myself for a law-and-order speech.

Ding, dong.

Saved by the bell. "I should get that."

Mother's brows rose. Why was I answering my own door?

"Everyone but me has a job," I explained.

"You told Bruce Alexander you had a million things to do."

"I lied."

She nodded, almost as if she approved. I hoped her hungover brain didn't remember I'd told her about the same nonexistent million.

We walked to the front door together.

"I should go." She patted her hair. "But I'll see you tonight. Call me if you need anything." Mother pressed her fingers against her temples as if my impending wedding worsened her headache.

We both knew I'd never make that call. "Of course." I gave her a tight smile and quick hug, then opened the front door.

Detective Peters and a man I didn't know waited on the stoop.

Both Mother and Peters recoiled as if I'd presented each of them with the person they'd least like to see. Perhaps I had.

Mother's brows lifted to her hairline, and she rubbed her chin as if she were mentally auditioning snide remarks about Peters' raincoat or mustache or general appearance.

Peters glared.

Mother's presence had never—not once—enhanced my

experience with the police. "Go," I told her. "We'll see you tonight."

She replied with a regal nod.

The men on the stoop stepped aside, and Mother swanned past them.

With Mother safely out the door, I offered a smile. "Won't you please come in?"

Peters entered my home and grunted at me.

The stranger, a man of medium height, unruly brown hair threaded with silver, and piercing gray eyes, held out his hand. "I'm Dan Rogan. Pleasure to meet you."

"Likewise, Detective Rogan."

"Call me Dan." He had a friendly smile. Disarming. Almost too sweet to belong to a homicide detective.

"Call me Ellison."

Peters scowled at both of us. "Is Jones here?"

"No. He's at the Alameda."

Peters glowered, as if I'd plotted this latest inconvenience just to annoy him. "Jones left a message. Said our cases—" he jerked a thumb at Dan "—might be related, but he's not answering pages."

"Anarchy turned in the pager for the next two weeks." I ignored Peters's death glare. "I know why he called."

"Why is that?" Peters grumbled.

"Because of what Prudence told me."

"Who's Prudence?" asked Dan.

"She's a long story." Maybe I could improve Peters's mood before I told it. "Have you had lunch? There's food in the kitchen."

"Aggie made it?" asked Peters.

"I think so. Possibly Mac."

"Long as it wasn't you," he replied.

Oh dear Lord. The man's favorite restaurant was shuttered for multiple health notations, and he was insulting my cooking?

"Little known fact." Dan flashed a second disarming smile. "Peters was raised by wolves."

"That explains so much."

Dan laughed, Peters marinated in ire, and I led them to the kitchen.

The men filled their plates, and I refreshed my iced tea. "I'm afraid we'll have to chat in the study. It's the only room not crawling with florists."

My late husband's study steadfastly refused redecoration. The whole room reminded me of Henry, and I avoided it whenever possible.

Dan settled into a club chair and asked, "Prudence?"

I perched on the edge of the desk. "Right. Prudence Davies. We don't like each other."

"Why not?"

"The Davies woman slept with her—" Peters indicated me with the pointy end of his sandwich "—late husband."

"That's not a long story," Dan replied.

I glanced at my watch. "I'm getting married in six hours. We don't have time for the whole sordid tale. Suffice to say, it's odd that she approached me."

Dan grinned. "What did she say?"

"She told me Lilly Frasier was blackmailing someone into proposing her and her husband for club membership." I waited for a reaction.

Both men stared at me. Blankly.

"I actually believe her." Not always true when Prudence spoke. "I heard a rumor about it from Libba, who heard it from Billie Weston."

They still didn't respond. Didn't react.

It was as if I spoke in a foreign language, one of I had no hope of learning, like Mandarin or Arabic.

I tried again. "Lilly wasn't well liked. No one would propose the Frasiers unless they had to."

Still no reaction.

"The Frasiers's admission was far from a given." If anything, the opposite. "None of the men with whom Trip Frasier does business would risk putting the couple up for membership." No one wanted the embarrassment of a failed proposal. "Trust me, this is a big deal."

The two men exchanged a look. A look that said I'd lost my mind.

"How do you know they wouldn't get in?" asked Dan.

How to explain? That some people fit and others did not was something Mother might say. "I just know."

Peters put down his sandwich and stared at me. "Are you on some super-secret membership committee?"

"No."

He responded with an I-don't-believe-you brow lift and poorly concealed glee. "You are!"

The desk's edge cut into the back of my legs. I pushed away and stood straight. "I am not. First off, I'm a woman. There are no women on the committee." There should be. "Our husbands are the members."

"Your husband is dead." Peters leaned back in his chair as if he'd won an argument and there was nothing left to say.

"Fair point. But I'm too artsy for the membership committee."

Dan frowned. "What does that mean?"

I took a sip of iced tea. "I'm an artist and might harbor wild ideas like allowing single women to join the club."

He blinked.

"And if enough women held memberships, they might demand equal access to the golf course or insist on ordering a cocktail in the men's bar. It would be utter chaos."

Dan grinned.

Peters rolled his eyes.

I waited for the next question.

"Do you, or Prudence, have any proof Lilly Frasier was blackmailing Avery and Rose's killer?" Dan's piercing eyes fixed on my face.

"I do not. But I don't believe in coincidences."

"Neither do I." He wiped his mouth with a paper napkin. "The day you found Avery Stallard and Rose Reynolds, did you see anyone else at the thrift shop?"

Peters snickered. "Two of her friends were in the parking lot and she didn't notice them. Do you think she'd register a stranger?"

"No one I didn't mention," I replied to Dan, then turned to Peters. "I had other things on my mind. Also, it wasn't as if I expected to find a body."

"I don't know why not," said Peters. "You find them on a weekly basis."

"I do not."

"This week you found three in less than thirty-six hours."

I'd had enough of Peters's snark. "Max found Lilly."

"Who's Max?" asked Dan.

"Her dog." Peters's smile was chilly. "So you know, the dog counts as you finding the body."

I could have pointed out that Anarchy was with me. Instead, I stepped away from the desk, walked to the window, and crossed my arms. It was that or throttle Peters.

"Did Lilly have any interaction with the Stallards?" asked Dan. "Were they friends?"

"No."

"They're the ones with motives," said Peters.

"What about the man Avery tricked into getting her pregnant?" I wanted the Stallards, all of them, to be innocent.

"She wasn't pregnant," said Peters. "And David Wilson has an alibi. He was at a conference in Las Vegas when Avery Stallard died."

Drat. "So, the Stallards." Even as I said their name, something felt off, wrong, as if I were looking at things through a wonky lens. "Can you track Lilly's movements from the time of Avery and Rose's murders?" Could they discover what she knew?

Dan's gaze flickered. "We're trying."

Tap, tap.

"Come in," I called.

Anarchy opened the door, and I smiled. We'd only been apart for a few hours, but I'd missed him.

His face remained blank. Whatever he thought about finding me with two homicide detectives, he hid it well.

"Everything okay with Journey?" Unexpected nerves made my voice too high.

"Fine." His expression softened. "How are you?"

"Dan and Detective Peters came looking for you. I just told them about my conversation with Prudence."

"I see." His gaze shifted to Peters. "A word?"

"Yeah." Peters struggled to rise from the too-deep club chair.

Anarchy watched, his face set in stone.

When Peters finally stood, the two left us.

"I guess best wishes are in order," said Dan.

"Thank you." What was wrong? Why did Anarchy need to speak with Peters?

"How did you and Jones meet?"

I suspected Dan already knew the answer. "Anarchy investigated my husband's murder."

"That's right." He grimaced. "Your husband, he was a blackmailer."

My heart skipped a beat. "That's not common knowledge."

Dan tilted his head as if I'd said something confusing.

"I have a daughter. Her life will be easier if Henry's sins aren't widely known."

He put the remains of his sandwich on his plate and stretched his legs out in front of him. "It just seems odd."

"What seems odd?"

"That you're intimately familiar with blackmail, come to us with a story about blackmail, and the person you say told you about this blackmail swears she hasn't spoken to you in weeks."

Two thoughts arrived in rapid succession.

First, Dan Rogan's friendly demeanor was a dastardly front.

Secondly, I wanted to kick Prudence Davies in her horse teeth.

"She's lying."

"Maybe." He pushed a potato chip around his plate. "But you found three bodies."

"Am I a suspect, Detective?"

"I wouldn't say that."

"What would you say?"

"You find an unimaginable number of bodies."

"Why would I kill any of those women?"

"No one accused you of murder."

True, but he'd hinted. And that hint felt like a threat.

Anarchy appeared in the doorway wearing a face like thunder. "Ellison?"

I hurried to him.

"You okay?" For long seconds, his gaze searched my face.

"Fine." My heart thumped too hard and fast, and anger swirled in my belly, but I smiled into his coffee-brown eyes.

We communicated silently.

I'm a suspect!

Rogan has nothing, so he's looking everywhere.

And Peters?

Anarchy's lips thinned. *I'll deal with Peters.* He shifted his gaze to Rogan and draped his arm around my shoulders. "Peters is waiting for you in the car."

Rogan nodded and stood. "Nice meeting you, Ellison." He put his plate on Henry's desk. "Thanks for the sandwich."

"I'll walk you to the door." I wanted him out of my house.

"No need. I can see myself out. I'm sure you two have lots to talk about."

When the front door closed behind Rogan, I sagged. "What the hell?"

"I'm sorry."

"It's not your fault." I rested my head against Anarchy's broad chest, took a calming breath, then forced myself to look into his eyes. "Peters doesn't like me, but surely he realizes I'm not a killer."

Anarchy's lips compressed to a razor-thin line.

"How will this affect you?" Would marrying me cost him the job he loved?

He frowned. "What do mean?"

"You're a detective. It can't be good for your career to be tied to a perennial suspect."

"You're not a real suspect."

"Funny, I sure feel like one."

"You were with me when Lilly Frasier drowned."

So I had an alibi for one of the murders. But Avery and Rose? When it came to the timeline and lacking an alibi and finding the bodies, I looked guilty. "It's as if Rogan and Peters thought I was trying to mislead them."

Anarchy didn't reply.

"They know I didn't kill Lilly. But would I hurt Avery and Rose?" My voice was approaching a pitch heard only by dogs.

"You wouldn't." By contrast, Anarchy sounded cool and in control.

"Peters and Rogan don't agree with you."

"Ellison, you're innocent. This will sort itself out."

"Will they let a murder suspect board a plane for Italy?"

"You're innocent."

"You keep saying that, but you don't answer my questions."

"Fine. There's a theory you had time to kill Avery and Rose. Also the murder weapon—"

"Henry's golf club."

"Exactly." He closed his eyes and a pained expression flashed across his face. "Yours were the only fingerprints."

"The killer wore gloves."

"Exactly.

"I had no reason to want them dead."

"I know, sweetheart."

My jaw ached and my eyes stung. "This is my wedding day. Our wedding day. We have to solve this."

"Is something wrong?"

We turned and looked at Aggie.

She read the answer on our faces. "You should eat." Aggie solved problems with food. "Have you had lunch?"

I nodded, and Anarchy said, "I ate with my sister."

Which meant salad. "Are you still hungry?" I asked. "Aggie has sandwiches made."

"I could eat."

"I'll fix you a plate." Aggie paused, and her gaze searched my face. "What else can I do?"

My chin wobbled. "I'm a suspect in Avery and Rose's murders."

Her sharp intake of breath was followed by a long hiss. "Seriously? That's ridiculous."

"Apparently not."

"Come to the kitchen. I'll get Anarchy's sandwich, then we'll figure out who did it." Aggie made finding a killer sound so easy.

"We'll be there in a minute," Anarchy replied.

I watched her walk to the kitchen with enough oomph in her stride to make her kaftan snap with each step. "Prudence lied. She told Rogan she hadn't talked to me."

"The woman is a menace." Anarchy's jaw didn't move when he spoke.

"Maybe she lied because I refused to hire her." It was a possibility. "Or maybe because she hates me. The thing is..." I ran my fingers through my hair and followed my thoughts down a winding path. "I think she was telling the truth. I need to call Billie Weston."

"Who?"

"Libba said Billie Weston told her about the Frasiers' proposal for club membership." I frowned at Henry's desk. "The club directory is in my desk." I grabbed Anarchy's hand and led him to the kitchen, where Aggie was putting the finishing touches on his lunch. "Be right back." I dashed into the family room and grabbed the directory from the top drawer.

"We'll be done soon," said Bob, the florist.

"You've transformed my house. It's never looked more lovely."

"I'm glad you like it."

In addition to the potted hydrangeas and palms, countless bouquets dotted the tables. Outside, the patio looked like a fairy garden.

"I love it." And not a single petal mattered.

With the directory clasped in my hand, I returned to the kitchen, looked up Billie's number, and dialed.

"Weston residence."

"This is Ellison Russell. May I please speak with Billie?"

"One moment, please." I heard a muffled voice call, "Mom, telephone." Then the click of another extension picking up.

"Hello."

"Billie, it's Ellison Russell."

"Still Russell?" Under different circumstances, the smile in her voice might have brought a smile to my lips.

"The wedding's tonight."

"And you're calling me? It must be important."

"I won't take but a minute of your time."

"Take all the time you want. You're the one with a million things to do."

Just one thing. I needed to solve a murder. "Libba mentioned the Frasiers were being proposed for club membership."

Billie let a few seconds pass. "I might have told her something about that. Things have changed since Lilly drowned."

"I don't suppose you know who proposed them?"

"No. Lilly just told me it would happen."

My stomach sank. "Any ideas?"

"I assumed the Gilchrists. They are next-door neighbors."

"Right." Hell would freeze over before Laura Gilchrist let Charles propose the Frasiers. Billie didn't have the answer.

"I'd ask around for you, but with Lilly gone..."

"No need," I replied. "I was just curious. If you hear anything…"

"You'll be the first to know. Best wishes to you."

"Thanks, Billie. I'll see you soon." I hung up the phone and faced Anarchy. "She didn't know."

"It was a good idea to call her."

Aggie rested her elbows on the kitchen island and leaned forward. "What's your working theory?"

"Lilly Frasier blackmailed Avery and Rose's killer into proposing her and her husband for club membership." It sounded farfetched. No wonder I was a suspect. There was actual evidence against me.

"It's a reasonable theory," said Aggie.

I could have kissed her.

Instead, I sank onto a stool and let my head fall into my hands.

"Then what?" she asked. "The killer drowned Lilly?"

It didn't sound farfetched. It sounded outlandish.

Anarchy rubbed a comforting circle on my back. "We'll figure this out."

"Figure what out?" asked Grace.

I groaned.

"What?" she demanded.

I lifted my head. "I'm a suspect."

"What kind of suspect?"

"Murder," I muttered.

She rolled her eyes. "Who thinks you'd commit a murder?"

"Peters."

"Well, that's just stupid. Anarchy, tell him Mom is innocent."

"I have."

"And?"

"He can't take my word for it. He has to investigate every angle."

She huffed her displeasure. "What about the wedding?" Her eyes narrowed. "You're not postponing?"

"Absolutely not." Anarchy's reply was instantaneous.

I glanced out the window at the enchanted patio, endured the unutterable pain of my heart shattering, and said, "Maybe we should."

CHAPTER SIXTEEN

"What madness is this?" Libba stood in the doorway from the hall with her hands on her hips and an I'm-going-to-be-your-maid-of-honor-or-heads-will-roll scowl on her face. She'd obviously heard me mention postponing the wedding.

Where had she come from? "When did you get here?"

"Answer the question, Ellison. Have you lost your ever-loving mind?"

Aggie got very busy wiping counters, and Grace studied her shoes.

"I'm a murder suspect."

Libba and Grace exchanged a look, then Libba rolled her eyes with Grace-like disdain. "Pish."

"Pish?"

"Your being a murder suspect is nothing new," she replied.

I opened my mouth to argue, but a hand closed around my wrist.

"Come with me." Anarchy tugged me toward the back door.

"Where are we going?"

"Outside." His shoulders were stiff, his mouth was tight, and the tic near his left eye danced a jig. Anarchy was furious. With me.

Three sets of wide eyes watched my irate fiancé drag me to the patio.

He stopped less than a foot from the archway laced with English ivy and flowers—the exact spot where we were supposed to exchange vows in a few hours—and glared at me. "Do you love me?"

How could he ask that? "Yes."

"Do you want to marry me?"

More than anything. "I can't destroy your career."

He shook his head, rejecting my answer. "Do you want to marry me? It's a simple yes or no question."

"No. It's not. How could I knowingly do something that might cost you your job?"

"It's just a job."

"It's what you always wanted."

"You're what I always wanted."

I closed my eyes against the pain I saw on his face. "You wanted to be a cop."

"Look at me." His voice was harsh.

I took a breath.

"Ellison, open your eyes and look at me." I opened my eyes, and Anarchy gazed into them. "What I've always wanted is a partner who saw me, really saw me, and still wanted to grow old with me. I wanted hand holding and favorite bottles of wine, after-dinner walks, and shared coffee in the morning. I wanted the certainty I'd found my home. And when I say 'home,' I don't mean a place, but a person. You. I found all that with you."

This man. Tears welled and spilled down my cheeks.

"You didn't kill those women. Peters knows it."

"And Rogan?"

Anarchy's expression darkened. "He'll figure it out."

"Your job—"

"Doesn't matter." He wiped the tears from my cheeks, and it took everything I had not to lean into his touch.

His job mattered. To him. To me. "If our places were reversed and marrying me meant I might never paint again, what would you do?"

Anarchy raked his fingers through his hair. "Would you paint if you weren't paid for your paintings?"

"Yes." My voice was small but sure.

"No way would I visit crime scenes or tell people their loved ones are gone if I didn't get paid. Being a painter is what you are. Being a cop is what I do. Also, you're innocent. No one cares if I marry an innocent woman."

I had an argument, a good one, ready on my tongue, but Anarchy pressed a finger against my lips. "Please, Ellison, marry me. Tonight. As we planned." His gaze scanned the patio. "I love you with my whole heart, and it would be a crying shame for all these flowers to go to waste."

How could I say no? "You're sure?"

"I've never been surer of anything." His arms circled my back and pulled me close.

I melted into him.

"Mom!"

I turned my head away from what might have been the best, most romantic kiss in the history of kisses. "Yes?"

"Celeste is here. She wants to talk to you."

I stiffened. "She's here?"

"I literally just said that."

"Now?"

"Celeste is here. Now. She wants to talk to you."

"Be nice to me. It's my wedding day, and I'm emotional."

"You think?" Sarcasm dripped from Grace's voice.

"You don't have to talk to my mom," said Anarchy.

"I can't refuse to see your mother."

"I can go with you."

I suspected whatever Celeste came to say would remain unspoken in her son's presence. "Tempting offer."

"But?"

"I don't know your mother well, but she seems like the type of woman who'll have her say." I could listen now or watch her stand when the minister asked if anyone had just cause. "Either now, at the wedding, or at the reception."

Anarchy's mouth brushed against my ear. "No matter what she says, no matter what she does, in three hours, I will make you my wife."

Who could resist that?

We walked into the kitchen together.

"I'm still the maid of honor?" Libba smirked.

"Yes."

"Wedding day jitters," said Aggie. "Completely understandable."

Jitters? The fear I might be bad for Anarchy's career was worse than jitters. But I'd offered him an out, and he seemed determined to marry me. I was done trying to convince him otherwise.

"Where is my mother?" Anarchy asked.

"In the living room," Aggie replied.

I took a step toward the front hall, but Anarchy stopped me with a hand on my arm. "You're sure you don't want me to come?"

"Let me see what she wants."

"Call if you need me."

I walked down the hallway and slipped into the living room. "Celeste."

Anarchy's mother sat in my favorite wingback chair with her hands folded in her lap.

"May I offer you a drink?"

"Your maid already asked."

"I don't have a maid."

She pursed her lips.

"Aggie is my housekeeper and she's family."

"Family who sleeps in the maid's room, cleans your house, does your laundry, and cooks your meals."

That argument wouldn't end well for either of us. "What do you want to talk about, Celeste?"

"I came to apologize."

"For what?"

She grimaced, and her face settled into a pained expression. "River says you make Anarchy happy."

I took a seat on the sofa and waited for more.

Celeste said nothing. Long seconds passed, and I glanced at my watch.

"Am I keeping you?" Her gaze fixed on Big Blue.

"Well, I am getting married in a few hours." Maybe she'd believe I had a million things to do.

"Do you?"

I blinked. Have a million things? Not really. "Do I what?"

"Make him happy?"

"I try." A soft smile touched my lips. "He makes me happy."

She nodded. Once. "Maybe you do make him happy. He gave you his grandmother's ring. May I see your studio?"

I stared at her. No good would come of this. Celeste looked down her nose at pretty art and artists who painted beauty rather than pain. Nothing in my studio would impress her.

"Please?"

How could I refuse? I stood. "It's on the third floor."

Celeste followed me up two flights of stairs, and we paused in the center of my studio. I breathed comforting smells, gesso and turpentine and paint, let my fingers trail across a stack of books about my favorite artists, and picked up a charcoal and returned it to a cup of pencils.

Celeste parked herself in front of an easel and stared at the canvas. "You're surprisingly good."

I ignored the backhanded portion of her compliment. "Thank you."

"But your art is too pretty." I saw that coming. "Real art challenges, pushes boundaries, reveals hidden truths. You could make a difference. Instead you daub pretty pablum."

Annoyance stiffened my spine. "Real art also acts as a balm to the soul, brings joy, and offers comfort."

Her face tightened, and she scowled at the canvas as if her gaze might encourage the pretty still life to spontaneously combust.

"Celeste, I cede that art can and should do all the things you said, but it should also celebrate beauty. I'd rather spend an hour looking at a Monet than a de Kooning."

She muttered something. I was fairly certain it wasn't flattering.

Why did I bother? Celeste found my work humdrum and pedestrian. She found me humdrum and pedestrian. I forced a pleasant expression. "Art is subjective."

Another mutter. Definitely insulting.

Still, I had to try. "When I look at de Kooning's Woman I, I see misogyny. I bet you see a woman constrained by society or the exploration of the grotesque. Same painting, vastly different views."

"The artist has a viewpoint. Art is not subjective."

Art was completely subjective, and I felt honor bound to defend my point. "Are Warhol's Campbell Soup Cans a commentary on mass production or simply paintings of cans of soup? What's more, are they even good?"

She shifted her scowl my way. "Don't be simplistic."

"I'm not." She was being stubborn. "There's more than one way to look at—" A notion wavered like a mirage on a sunny highway. I couldn't see it clearly, but I was certain that beneath the shimmer I'd find one of Celeste's unpleasant hidden truths.

"What?" she snapped. "Are you constipated?"

I held up a finger. "Give me a minute." The thought—the important thought—danced at the edge of my brain. With a moment's silence, I might actually think it.

"You look constipated." Celeste gave me another ten seconds and an aggrieved huff, then turned on her heel and stormed downstairs.

The almost-realized idea dissipated like mist, and I muttered a curse of my own.

Safe to say, my relationship with my mother-in-law would never be warm. Also, she was worse at apologizing than Mother. I took a final look around my studio, then followed her.

Anarchy waited for me in the foyer.

"Is she gone?" Had I annoyed her so thoroughly she hadn't bothered with a goodbye?

"She is. What did she say?"

"She came to apologize."

"My mother? Did she actually tell you she was sorry?"

"Strictly speaking, no. She asked if I made you happy, then told me my painting is surprisingly good."

Anarchy winced. "Well, I apologize." He kissed my nose. "I'm sorry for my mother." Another kiss. "My father."

I tilted my head, so his next kiss landed on my lips.

"My brother." His lips were both firm and soft. "My sister." Another delicious kiss. "And anything they say or do to annoy you."

I liked this game. I lifted up on tiptoes and kissed him. "I'm sorry for Mother."

"That apology requires more than one kiss."

I happily complied.

"Break it up, you two," said Libba.

"If we ignore her, maybe she'll leave."

"I can hear you, Ellison."

"I know."

"You've got to get ready."

"I am ready."

"You're ready for a trip to the grocery store, not a wedding."

"She looks beautiful to me," said Anarchy.

"What do you know? You're crazy in love."

Libba grabbed my right hand and pulled me from Anarchy's embrace. "Come on. We have serious work to do."

"Don't you have to get ready?"

"Please." She waved away my paltry question. "I have that covered. Will you come willingly, or do I have to drag you?"

"Go," said Anarchy. "I'll see you soon."

"Nope," said Libba. "You two have already flaunted not seeing the bride on her wedding day. You don't get to see her again until she meets you on the patio." She glanced at our joined hands and gasped. "Holy smokes! Where did that boulder come from?"

Big Blue sparkled in the late afternoon light.

"My wedding gift from Anarchy."

"Yet another reason to marry him. Come with me. Now."

I let Libba lead me to my bedroom, where she made me wash my face. She held out her hand. "Hand it over."

I put Big Blue in her palm.

"Wow. Just wow." Her eyes narrowed. "Are you over your drama?"

"I'm still a murder suspect. But Anarchy doesn't care."

"Duh. That man adores you. And he knows you're innocent."

She returned Big Blue, and I slipped the ring onto my finger. "Peters has doubts."

"When it comes to you, Peters looks at things all wrong."

The elusive thought returned, but this time I grabbed onto it, examined it, let it steal my breath.

"What's wrong?" Libba demanded. "You just went pale."

"How well did you know Rose?"

"Rose?"

"From the thrift shop."

"Oh. Rose. I knew her to speak to. Why?"

"Everyone has focused on Avery as the primary victim."

"Because every single member of her family had a good reason to want her dead."

"True. But what if Rose was the primary target?"

"Then why beat Avery with a golf club?"

"Avery's death was a crime of passion, and unlucky Rose happened to be there. That's what we've all believed. Maybe the killer wanted everyone focused on Avery."

"Why would someone kill Rose? She was single. She managed a thrift shop. She..." Libba bit the tip of her pointer finger.

"She what?"

"Nothing. That's all I know about her."

"She didn't want to retire."

"Good Lord. Why not?" Libba avoided the thrift shop. She found last year's fashions hanging on waxed rods terribly depressing.

"She didn't have enough saved, and her annuities didn't mature for another two years."

"She had annuities? Who's her heir?"

"I assume her sister or her niece." I frowned. "I met her family, and they seemed genuinely heartbroken by her death."

"If not for money, why kill her?" She shook her head. "I can't see her engendering the kind of emotion needed for murder."

"I'm sure I'm right." I headed for the door.

"Whoa there." Libba grabbed my wrist. "Where do you think you're going?"

"To tell Anarchy."

"Not a chance."

"This is murder."

"This is your wedding day. You can tell him later." She pointed to a chair set next to the window. A folding card table sat next to it and makeup covered the table's surface. "Right now, we're doing your face."

"It will take two minutes."

"Not falling for that, Ellison. You'll tell him, then you'll decide to go investigate, lose track of time, and walk down the aisle with no makeup."

Brnng, brnng.

"Let it ring." She pointed to the chair.

Brnng, brnng.

"I mean it."

Brnng, brnng.

"Mom." Grace popped her head into my room. "Granna needs to talk to you."

Libba sighed her annoyance. "No."

"She says it's important."

I picked up the receiver. "Hello."

"Will Peters be at your wedding?"

"I think so."

"You don't know?"

If he planned on arresting me or forbidding me from traveling to Italy, he might skip the ceremony. "What do you need, Mother?"

"He's investigating the murders at the thrift shop, yes?"

"Yes."

"Well, your father isn't happy with me. He wants those registration papers, and he wants them yesterday. Can Peters get them for me?"

I imagined asking Peters to fetch registration papers from a crime scene and shuddered. "Where would he look?"

"The thrift shop."

"It's a big place, Mother."

"I don't need your sarcasm. Not when your father is

perturbed with me. Tell him he can look in Rose's desk, the safe, the cash register."

Peters's reaction to such a directive might lead to my murder. "I'll let you tell him."

"Ellison." She made my name a warning.

"Nope. Not doing it. You accidentally gave the papers away. You can ask for them back.

"Fine." She hung up. With force.

I collapsed into the chair Libba set out for me. "Is there a reason we're not doing this in the bathroom?"

"You're not getting married in a bathroom. This way, we have natural light."

I glanced out the window. "Libba?"

"Mhmm?" She looked up from picking a bottle of foundation.

"Why is there a pickup truck filled with cases of liquor in my driveway?"

"You're the one getting married."

"They're unloading the cases."

She wouldn't meet my gaze.

Suspicion twisted in my gut. "What did you do?"

"Me?" She sounded too innocent.

Outside, Mac's catering van pulled into the drive, bypassed the circle portion, and disappeared beyond the side of the house.

"I mean it, Libba. What's going on?"

"It's a surprise."

"I hate surprises."

"You won't hate this one." Her eyes went shifty.

"Tell me now."

"Nope."

"Libba." I stood.

"Where are you going?"

"To tell the deliverymen to take the liquor back."

"You can't!"

"Why not?"

"You'll ruin the surprise."

"I hate surprises."

"You keep saying that."

"Because it's true."

"Fine."

I waited with crossed arms.

"Grace and I might have asked a few extra guests to your reception."

Dread settled on my shoulders. "How many?"

"A few."

"Eight? Ten? Twenty?"

Libba stared out the window.

"Thirty?"

"A humph," she mumbled.

"I'm sorry. I didn't understand what you said." I did understand, but I couldn't believe it.

"A hundred." Her eyes were defiant.

"You asked a hundred people to my home? I'm leaving for Italy tomorrow."

She shrugged.

"Who knows about this?" I wanted a list.

"Grace and Aggie and—" her shifty gaze fixed on a spot over my left shoulder "—and Frances."

"So my mother, my daughter, and my best friend conspired against me."

"We didn't conspire! This is why we didn't tell you."

"If I'd wanted a hundred people at my reception, I would have invited them!"

"It'll be fun."

"No wonder you had a conniption when I talked about postponing. 'What madness is this?'" I mimicked. "It wasn't about being my maid of honor, you didn't want to cancel a party."

"That's not fair."

"But it's true."

"Maybe a little, but it was more about being your maid of honor and seeing you happily married." She gave me the hairy eyeball. "There's nothing you can do. You might as well sit down and let me fix your makeup."

How could I uninvite a hundred people in time? Especially when I didn't have the guest list. I sighed. "You're gloating."

"Moi?" She pressed her fingertips to her chest.

"Yes, you." I resumed my seat. "I want light makeup. A natural look. No warpaint."

She pouted.

"You're on thin ice."

"Fine." She caught her upper lip in her teeth and got to work.

CHAPTER SEVENTEEN

"Mom, you look beautiful." High praise from a teenager.

With Anarchy's pence safely stashed in my shoe, I looked up and saw her eyes shimmering with tears. I gave her a wobbly smile and opened my arms for a hug.

Grace stepped into my embrace. Her hair smelled like apples, her skin smelled like Love's Baby Soft, and her lips smelled like her cherry-flavored gloss. I breathed her in.

"I'm so happy for you." Her whisper tickled my ear.

"Me, too."

"You're all set?" She stepped back for a last look.

"The ring is new and blue." It sparkled like a mountain lake. "The earrings are Libba's." She'd loaned me diamond studs. "The bracelet is old." I held out my wrist and admired the pearl bracelet with a diamond clasp Daddy gave me when I graduated high school.

"Are you nervous?" she asked.

"A little bit. Are you?"

She frowned. "Why would I be nervous?"

"You let Libba talk you into a big reception."

A deep rose hue colored her cheeks. "Oh. That."

"That." My voice was as dry as old bones.

She pulled at the neckline of her pretty blue dress. "How did you find out?"

"I saw the liquor delivery. Since when are you in league with Libba?"

"Did I mention you look beautiful?"

"You did. How could you, Grace?"

She held out her hands in appeal. "Have you tried telling Libba no? It's not easy."

It was nearly impossible. "What about Aggie?"

"Don't blame Aggie. It's not her fault. Libba only told her after she'd invited everyone. And you know how Aggie is. The thought of running out of food or clean glasses had her on the phone with Mac for more canapés and the rental company for additional service-ware."

"How many people did Libba invite?" I held my breath.

"A hundred."

I exhaled. Libba hadn't lied to me. Much.

"Are you mad?"

"I'm too happy to be mad." Happy was a pale word for the joy bubbling in my soul. It left no room for other emotions.

Outside, Gayla strummed the beginning chords of Pachelbel's "Canon in D."

"That's our cue." Grace's eyes didn't shimmer, they welled. "Are you ready?"

I smoothed my dress. "I am."

We stepped onto the patio, and my gaze sought Anarchy.

He stood in front of the archway and pressed his palm to his mouth as if he couldn't believe his luck. The fading light gilded his hair, and his eyes brimmed with love.

My heart did cartwheels in my chest. I was the lucky one.

Grace took my hand. "Let's do this."

I clutched my bouquet, breathed in the scents of hyacinth

and freesia, and floated down the short aisle. Then I gave my bouquet to Libba and took my spot next to Anarchy.

This felt right. My worries—being a murder suspect and our troublesome mothers—didn't matter. This—Anarchy and me—was right. Better than right. Together, we were perfect.

Reverend Phillips talked. I barely listened. I couldn't focus on anyone or anything but the man who was minutes away from being my husband.

The ceremony blurred, and I was almost surprised when Anarchy took my hand. "Ellison, I give you this ring as a symbol of my vow, and with all that I am, and all that I have. I honor you, in the name of the Father, and of the Son, and of the Holy Spirit."

I heard Celeste squawk. The woman probably worshipped a goddess.

Then it was my turn. "Anarchy, I give you this ring as a symbol of my vow, and with all that I am, and with all that I have. I honor you, in the name of the Father, and of the Son, and of the Holy Spirit."

Reverend Phillips beamed and joined our hands. "Now that Ellison and Anarchy have given themselves to each other by solemn vows, with the joining of hands and the giving and receiving of rings, I pronounce that they are husband and wife."

I was grateful Libba talked me into waterproof mascara. The world swam behind my tears. How was it possible to be so happy?

"You may kiss your bride."

Anarchy, my husband, kissed me. His warm lips against mine sent bottle rockets and sparklers and Roman candles careening through my veins. This was more than a kiss. It was today and tomorrow and forever. It was joy and promise and hope. The kiss was all that we were together.

My arm snaked around his neck. I wanted the kiss to last forever.

Reverend Phillips cleared his throat, our families chuckled, and Anarchy and I separated.

Well, our lips separated. Our gazes remained linked.

If my past had led me to this moment, then every jaw-jarring bump in the road had been worth it. I saw a lifetime in Anarchy's eyes.

"I present to you, Mr. and Mrs. Anarchy Jones."

Everyone clapped, and we walked down the aisle and entered the house through the family room doors. The room was filled with flowers and someone had set a bar in the corner.

"Champagne, Mrs. Jones?" Anarchy's eyes danced.

"Please." My face ached from smiling too much.

"We need you outside for pictures," said Mother, who'd followed us inside.

"We need a moment alone, Frances."

Mother blinked.

Anarchy handed me a flute filled with Champagne, took his own glass, and whispered, "To us. To a lifetime of love and happiness. To Italy."

We clinked glasses and drank.

"Ellison!" Mother didn't appreciate being put off. "The photographer is waiting."

"She won't stop," I whispered.

Anarchy chuckled softly. "I don't need photographs. I'll never forget a single second of this night."

"Swoony."

His smile gained a predatory edge. "I'll show you swoony."

Heat rose from my toes. "Can't wait."

"Ellison Walford Russell...Jones, your family is waiting for you. Yours too, Anarchy."

He grinned. "Do we have to go?"

My heart flipped. "Grace's children might be interested in the photographs. Also, it's best not to antagonize the dragon."

"Fine," Anarchy ceded. "But I can't wait to have you to myself."

Amen.

We went outside and posed in front of the archway, the hydrangeas, and the sunset. We took pictures of the two of us, then pulled Grace into the frame. Anarchy took pictures with his family. I took pictures with mine—with Mother and Daddy, with Marjorie and Karma, with Aunt Sis and Gordon. Then I took pictures with Libba. So many pictures despite, or maybe because of, Mother and Celeste's opposing directions.

When Anarchy had enough, he pulled me away, and we returned to the bar for more Champagne. He eyed the mind-boggling number of bottles and the huge stack of glasses.

"What's going on?"

"Turns out Libba invited extra people."

He rubbed the back of his neck. "Why am I not surprised? Who did she invite?"

"No idea."

He eyed a case of gin. "How many?"

"A humph," I mumbled.

"How many?"

"A hundred."

"Fun." He sounded sincere.

"Fun?" Had marriage addled his brain?

"Our wedding is an occasion worth celebrating."

"I love you."

He kissed me. "Love you too, Mrs. Jones."

Ding, dong.

"And so it begins." I couldn't be mad at Libba. Tonight, I couldn't be mad at anyone.

Within minutes, the house filled with people.

"Ellison, you're gorgeous, and that dress is stunning." Jinx pulled me into a tight hug. "So happy for you."

I'd never admit it, but I was glad Libba had gone behind my

back. In addition to our families, many of my favorite people had come to celebrate our wedding.

"When do you leave for Italy?" she asked. "Early flight?"

"No. With Marjorie, Karma, and Anarchy's family traveling to join us, we couldn't just disappear. We're hosting a brunch tomorrow morning. Our plane leaves later in the afternoon."

"You're a good woman." She glanced toward Mother. "If it were me, I'd be in the air before dawn."

I searched for and found Celeste in the crowd. She was waving an empty Champagne flute in my neighbor Margaret Hamilton's face. Leaving early was tempting.

Laura and Charles Gilchrist stood nearby, waiting their turn to wish me well. But as long as I had Jinx and her gold mine of knowledge handy, I had questions.

"Did you hear anything about the Frasiers being proposed for membership at the club?"

She wrinkled her nose. "A little bird might have mentioned it. I suppose it's a moot point now."

"Any idea who Lilly lined up to propose them?"

She pursed her lips. "Not to speak ill of the dead, but Lilly was a fool to tell anyone. The likelihood they'd get in was microscopic."

"Maybe she had an in with the membership committee."

The tilt of Jinx's head and the calculation in her eyes said the possibility had merit. "Who's here from the committee? We'll find out." She scanned the room, and her gaze landed on Charles Gilchrist. "Charles will know." She waved him over.

"Good evening, Jinx." He bent and kissed my cheek. "Ellison, you look lovely."

"Thank you. And thank you for being part of my surprise reception. I'm so glad you and Laura are here."

Laura took my hand and squeezed. "You're glowing."

"I'm happy."

Jinx wrested control of the conversation. "Ellison and I were just chatting about the membership committee at the club."

Laura drew her brows. "Why?"

"There's a rumor going around that someone proposed the Frasiers." I pretended not to see Mother waving in my direction.

"Well, it wasn't us. That woman was a terrible neighbor."

"Ellison thinks she had an in with the committee," said Jinx.

Laura narrowed her eyes. "Doubtful. Any man who proposed that woman and her husband for membership would need a good divorce attorney."

Jinx flashed a sharp smile. "Did you hear anything, Charles? Are you still on the committee?"

"I didn't hear a word, and you know that committee is secret."

Curiosity brightened Jinx's eyes, and she tapped her chin. "An open secret." If Charles wouldn't tell us, she'd find someone who would. "Ellison's got me wondering about the sponsor. Lilly wasn't popular. If anything, the opposite." Lilly had used people as stepping stones in her pursuit of social prominence. A strategy that never worked.

"She was certain she and Trip would receive an invitation to join," I added. "Almost as if approval were a foregone conclusion."

"She was delusional." Laura's voice was unusually sharp.

"I don't think she was." I ignored Mother's attempts to catch my eye. "I think she had leverage."

My friends stared at me as if I'd grown another head.

Mother cut into our little group and nodded at Jinx and Laura and Charles. "So glad you could join us this evening. Ellison, you're needed in the dining room." Exasperation tinged her voice.

"The dining room?"

"Yes, Ellison. The cake. You and Anarchy need to cut the cake."

I excused myself to Jinx and the Gilchrists, then followed her into the dining room, where my jaw dropped.

The cake.

I'd requested two simple layers, vanilla icing, and lemon curd filling.

The massive cake in front of me had four layers, buttercream frosting, and edible gold-leaf decoration. There was nothing simple about it.

"Wow," I murmured.

Anarchy joined me at the cake table, and Mother watched as his warm hand swallowed mine. Together, we clasped a silver knife and cut through the gold-filigreed base tier.

A server helped us plate a slice, and Anarchy fed me a bite. White cake with lemon curd filling. At least that hadn't changed from the cake Aggie and I had planned.

I fed Anarchy his bite and the photographers snapped pictures.

"Not bad," he said. "Did Aggie make it?"

"We discussed it, but I'm not sure she has an oven big enough for something of this scale." I glanced at the laden dining room table. "I don't know how they pulled this off." In addition to a four-layer cake, there was food for a hundred-plus guests, a band, an army of service staff, and enough liquor to see us through Christmas.

A server took over the cake cutting, and Mother claimed our attention. "Time for your first dance."

Oh good Lord. When had she become a wedding coordinator?

"Easier not to argue," Anarchy whispered.

He was a fast learner.

I had years of practice. "Now? Can't we slow down and enjoy the party?"

"Yours is the first dance, Ellison."

"I didn't ask for a band."

"Be that as it may."

I crossed my arms.

Mother pursed her lips. "Do this, and I'll leave you alone for the rest of the evening."

"Promise?"

"I just said I'd leave you alone."

"Cross your heart?"

"Ellison." Her voice held a warning.

I hid a smile. "Pinky promise?"

"Fine. You win. I promise not to disturb your evening."

A small victory, but the first of my married life. I'd take it.

We followed Mother outside, where the chairs used during the ceremony now surrounded café tables and a trio with a singer had instruments set in front of the flowered arch. Anarchy and I took our places in the center of the impromptu dance floor.

"Did you pick a song?" he asked.

"I didn't know we'd have a band."

Anarchy's hand on the small of my back made me shiver, and I smiled up at him as the little band played "Isn't it Romantic."

"Did Libba pick this?" he whispered in my ear.

"No. If Libba picked a song, we'd be dancing to 'You Ain't Seen Nothing Yet.' This is Mother's selection."

The song ended, Daddy cut in, and the band launched into a better-than-average version of Natalie Cole's "This Will Be."

Daddy smiled at me with three-martini eyes. "Happy?"

"Ecstatic."

"He's a good man. He'll take care of you."

I'd given up trying to convince my father I didn't need a man as a caretaker. Tonight was for joy, not arguments about female empowerment. I tamped down a sassy reply and glanced at Anarchy, who was dancing with Mother. "He will."

"I'm counting on it."

More couples joined us on the dance floor.

When the song ended, Anarchy asked his mother to dance. Since Oscar was nowhere in sight, I went in search of Champagne.

As I approached the bar, someone tapped me on the shoulder.

I turned. "Dot! I'm so glad you're here."

"You look fabulous."

"Thank you."

"I love your dress."

"Swanson's."

She frowned, then caught her lower lip in her teeth. "I hate to take you away from your party, but is there somewhere we can talk?"

"Tonight?"

"It's important."

"Hen—" The room no longer belonged to Henry. "The study is empty."

Tonight, in honor of the party, we'd opened the pocket doors between the living and family rooms. Dot and I passed through them, then cut through a room crowded with friends. Each one wanted a word, offered a blessing, or complimented my dress. It took fifteen minutes to reach the front hall.

Compared to the flowers and Champagne and laughing people who filled the rest of the house, the study seemed particularly gloomy. Even ominous.

Dot drank deeply of whatever was in her highball, and it occurred to me I was alone with a murder suspect. It had happened before, and it seldom ended well.

"What can I do for you, Dot?" I smiled brightly.

Dot stared at the carpet. "Suppose I had information..."

"About the murders?"

She nodded.

"You know who killed Avery and Rose?" Did she suspect her sister? Her brother? Her father?

"Maybe. Possibly." She took another drink. "I think so." Misery weighted her words.

"Who?"

She glanced toward the closed door. "If I tell you, you can't tell anyone."

"Dot, I can't keep secrets from Anarchy."

Her lips pinched. "It's not his case."

"It's his partner's case."

She collapsed into a chair, took another long sip, then stared at her glass as if she couldn't figure out how it was empty. "I don't know what to do."

"Two women are dead." Three if we counted Lilly. Dot should share the information. If not with me, then with the police.

"I think I know, but what if I'm wrong?"

"Do you have evidence?"

"Not evidence." She picked at the fabric of her dress. "I may have seen someone at the thrift shop."

"And you're just remembering?" Sudden recall after her lies wasn't exactly convincing.

She stiffened at my tone. "This is the worst. I need another drink." She struggled to her feet. "I need to think about this."

"You should tell the police."

She swayed and hit me with a belligerent glare. "Maybe I will."

"I'm here if you need me."

"Thank you, Ellison. You're a good friend."

She swayed again and clutched the desk to keep herself upright.

"Dot, did Zane drive tonight?"

Her face scrunched, and she nodded. "He's around somewhere."

That was a relief. With more liquor than blood in her veins, Dot shouldn't be behind the wheel of a car.

She staggered into the foyer, then disappeared into the living room.

I lingered in the study. Should I tell Anarchy about the conversation I'd just had, or could we enjoy this night—our night—without the shadow of a murder investigation?

It was selfish, but it was also my wedding night. I'd tell him in the morning.

The evening passed in a Champagne-flavored blur of laughter and dancing and love.

Just before midnight, Anarchy found me. "We're leaving."

"What? Why? Where are we going?"

"I booked us a suite at the Alameda. Aggie packed you an overnight bag."

"But why?" His parents were staying at the Alameda.

"It's the closest hotel, and I'm not spending our wedding night with a party raging downstairs." The party had thinned, but the serious drinkers were doing their best to empty the bottles.

I blushed like a girl.

He brushed a promise-filled kiss across my lips. "Come on, Mrs. Jones. Let's tell Grace and Aggie good night. Then it's time to start our life together."

CHAPTER EIGHTEEN

Brnng, brnng.

I pulled the sheets over my head, burrowed deeper into the hotel's comfortable bed, and groaned. Who could be calling us?

Brnng, brnng.

"Hello," Anarchy grumbled.

I snuggled closer to him. "What time is it?"

When he didn't answer, I cracked my eyelids.

Delicate morning light snuck through a gap in the curtains.

"Give us an hour." He hung up.

My eyes opened all the way, and my heart fluttered. "What's wrong?" Who'd called? "Is Grace okay?"

"She's fine."

My stomach grumbled.

"Hungry?"

"I didn't have time to eat last night."

"Let's order coffee." He picked up the receiver, dialed room service, and ordered breakfast and a pot of coffee.

"Twenty minutes till they arrive." The predatory gleam in his eyes gave me shivers. "What shall we do while we wait?"

I ran my fingers through his mussed hair, then traced the line of his jaw. "I have a few ideas."

Twenty-five minutes later, I wore a satisfied smile, had bones made of rubber, and clutched a coffee cup. "Who called?"

"Aggie."

I lifted my brows.

"Dot Thompson didn't make it home last night."

One of our guests had gone missing? One who could potentially identify a killer? The coffee and toast in my stomach turned sour.

"Don't worry. She and her husband are—" Anarchy's face shuttered.

"Are what?"

"Having marital difficulties," he admitted. "It's possible she spent the night with someone else."

I stared at my new husband. "How do you know that?"

"She's a murder suspect. We dig."

I swallowed. "Dot came and found me last night. She said she had evidence. Sort of."

"What kind of evidence?"

"Something she saw at the thrift shop."

Annoyance flashed in his eyes. "So she changed her story. Again."

"Yes, but I believed her." And I'd said nothing. Was it my fault she'd gone missing? If I'd told Anarchy about our conversation, would she be safely home? "I should have told you last night."

He leaned over and kissed me. "I'm glad you didn't tell me. Last night was about us, not a murder investigation." He understood. He even agreed with my decision.

Guilt's sharp claws released their hold on my psyche.

"What time did you talk to her?"

"Shortly after we danced."

"Around nine thirty."

"Maybe a little later. We cut through the living room, which took forever."

His brows lifted. "Where did you go?"

"The study. She wanted to speak privately."

His lips thinned.

I took a bracing sip of coffee. "Dot is an old friend. I was perfectly safe."

Anarchy stood, and paced, and scowled. "It was a risk."

Daddy would be thrilled with my husband's protectiveness.

"She was drunk." As if gin made people docile.

He rubbed his eyes, then glanced at his new watch. "Brunch is in three hours. Our flight leaves at four." He took my hands, pulled me to my feet, and stared into my eyes. "We're getting on that plane. I don't care if Dot is still missing. I don't care if your mother is arrested for murder. I don't care if my mother is her victim. We're going on our honeymoon."

"No arguments here." I whole-heartedly agreed with his plan. "We should get dressed."

"Should we?" He leaned in for a slow kiss and robbed me of all resolve.

When we finally separated, ten minutes had ticked away.

"We should go." I was breathless.

"Yep." Anarchy didn't move.

"Dot is missing."

His fingertip trailed fire across my cheek. "Strictly speaking, Dot is not our problem."

"She was at our house last night."

He grinned.

"Why are you grinning?"

"You said 'our house.'"

Now I grinned too. "That's what it is."

He moved closer for another kiss, but I stopped him with a hand on his chest.

"Is Zane with Aggie and Grace?"

"He was when Aggie called."

"The poor man must be beside himself with worry."

"Given what I know, I doubt it." Anarchy knew entirely too much about my friend's marriage. "But, if you're worried, call Aggie."

I picked up the receiver and dialed.

"Jones residence."

That stopped me. Jones residence.

"Hello?"

"Aggie, it's Ellison." As eager as I was to ask about Zane and Dot, I had more important things to say. "Thank you for last night. I know it was Libba's idea and I also know who did the work. The party was spectacular."

"My pleasure. You made a beautiful bride."

"I'm grateful for everything you did. Is Zane Thompson at the house?"

"He left."

Good. At least Aggie and Grace weren't entertaining him. "Did he explain what's going on?"

"Apparently he and Mrs. Thompson had an argument when they arrived last night. She saw something or someone on the street and became upset. She insisted she needed to talk to you and came inside. When she couldn't locate you immediately, and this is according to Mr. Thompson, she drank copious amounts of gin. He also says she can't hold her liquor." He was right.

"Did he have any idea who or what she saw?"

"No. He's coming back. He insists on speaking with you."

Drat. "Anarchy and I will be on our way shortly."

"I'll have coffee waiting."

"You're the best." I dropped the receiver into its cradle. "We should get going."

Anarchy nodded, but the corners of his mouth turned down as if he could think of a better way to spend his morning.

I could, too.

With a sigh, I stepped into the bathroom and closed the door behind me.

Thirty minutes later, we were home and sitting at the kitchen island with mugs of hot fresh coffee in our hands. Aggie, who wore an eye-searing kaftan, wiped already clean counters.

"Did Zane say when he'd be back?" I asked.

"An hour." Aggie glanced at the clock on the stove. "He should be here."

The contents of my coffee cup called to me, and I drank. "Let's assume Dot spotted something or someone who jogged her memory." I drummed my fingers against the island's granite top. "Dot and her sister Tori were parked in front of the thrift shop when Avery and Rose died."

Aggie twisted her mouth into a you've-got-to-be-kidding-me expression.

"Go with it. Maybe she saw someone." I frowned. "Although, that's doubtful."

"Why?" asked Anarchy.

"With the exception of your family, Dot knew everyone here last night. If she saw one of the guests at the thrift shop, she'd have recognized them immediately. I got the impression she'd had some sort of epiphany."

"Then what did see?" asked Aggie.

"A car." It was an educated guess. "She recognized a car."

Aggie tilted her head. "How?"

"A bumper sticker, a decal, a dent, an unusual make or model, maybe just the license plate." They were all possibilities.

Anarchy nodded. "So she sees the car parked on the street outside your house and remembers seeing it at the thrift shop. Did she know who owned the car?"

I thought back to the odd conversation in the study. "I think so, but I wouldn't swear to it."

"Where do you suppose she went?" Aggie lifted the coffee pot, and I held out my mug for more.

I added cream, took a sip, and said, "I'm really hoping she didn't approach the car's owner."

The door to the back stairs opened, and Grace, who still wore pajamas, oozed into the kitchen. She grunted and helped herself to coffee. "What time is brunch?"

"Two hours," I replied.

She yawned and stretched and groused, "Who thought this brunch was a good idea?"

"Granna."

Another grunt. "Figures."

There was a motherly speech I could make—should make—about spending time with family and the importance of making the most of the time we had together. But when I thought about Celeste and Oscar, I drank my coffee and kept mum.

Grace sipped her coffee. "So? How's married life?"

Anarchy and I smiled at each other, and my face flushed with memories of last night and this morning.

My daughter screwed her eyes shut. "Ew. Just don't. Wait." She opened her eyes. "Didn't you stay at the Alameda last night? Aren't we having brunch there?" She didn't come out and ask what brought us home, but I read the question in her eyes.

"One of our guests didn't make it home last night."

"Who?"

"Dot Thompson."

She waved her hand. "Mrs. Thompson got a ride home."

Anarchy sat straighter. "What?"

"I saw her sitting on the stairs. Slumping. She was overserved and said she was waiting for a ride."

"Did she say with whom?" I asked.

"No."

It wasn't unusual for husbands to drop off and pick up their wives at the front door. Our driveway was long, especially for women in heels. But Dot hadn't been waiting on Zane.

"Her husband is looking for her."

"She got a ride with someone else." Grace was unconcerned. Rides were fluid things for teenagers.

Aggie, Anarchy, and I exchanged worried looks.

Was Dot buried in a shallow grave? "I should have lied."

Anarchy's brows rose. "Lied?"

"She wanted to tell me more about her suspicions, maybe even who killed Avery and Rose. I refused to keep what she told me a secret."

"Meaning?" he asked.

"I told her I'd tell you."

His expression warmed, and I wished we hadn't been in such an all-fire hurry to leave our hotel room. We shared a secret smile, one that came from my toes and reached the tip of my head.

"Do you have to do that?" Grace demanded.

Ding, dong.

"That must be Mr. Thompson," said Aggie. "I'll get it."

"I'll come with you." Grace rushed after her, as if her mother and stepfather's goo-goo eyes made her skin crawl.

I watched her disappearing back. "How much longer till our flight?"

"Too long."

Max barreled into the kitchen.

"Hey, buddy." I scratched behind his ears. "Guess it wasn't Zane."

Brnng, brnng.

Grace, who'd followed Max into the kitchen, answered the phone. "Russell—Jones res—hello." She listened. "I'll put her on the phone."

I held out my hand for the receiver, and she mouthed, "Sorry."

"Hello."

"Grace is old enough to know how to answer a phone." Mother's voice had a brittle, morning-after quality, as if she'd suddenly acquired a delicate constitution. Odd, when I hadn't seen her touch a drop of alcohol last night.

"Good morning."

"You sound chipper." She made chipper an accusation.

"I'm happy."

"It was a lovely party." Uh-oh. My radar pinged. Mother didn't offer cheap compliments.

"Libba and Aggie and Grace outdid themselves."

"Everyone had a marvelous time." Ping, ping, ping. What did she want?

"I looked for Peters but didn't see him."

Peters. Perhaps he sensed he'd hurt my feelings. Perhaps my friends made him uncomfortable. Perhaps he'd avoided Mother. He stayed at the reception only long enough to mumble his congratulations.

"Since I didn't have the opportunity to chat with him, you need to call him."

"Me?"

"Or your husband. I need those papers from the thrift shop."

Mother's comment parted the clouds in my brain, and a brilliant sunbeam of an idea smacked me across the face.

"Mother, I have to go."

"But—"

I hung up.

Grace's eyes widened. "Did you just hang up on Granna?"

"Whoops."

"You realize you have to see her in like two hours, right?" She shook her head as if I'd signed my own execution order.

Anarchy rose from his stool, his face creased with concern. "What is it, Ellison? What's wrong?"

"I just realized something."

He cocked a brow.

"I wondered if Rose was the real target but couldn't find a motive. What if someone accidentally donated something incriminating?"

"And Rose knew their secret?" asked Aggie.

I nodded. With enthusiasm. "Exactly. Rose was about to lose her job and needed enough money to live on until her annuities kicked in."

"Blackmail?" asked Grace.

"Then murder." I drained my coffee cup.

"Each and every member of the Stallard family had a motive." Anarchy was not convinced.

"I have a motive to kill Prudence." Sleeping with Henry was bad. Lying to the police about our conversation was worse. "Doesn't mean I'll do it."

"Even if you're right," he said. "We have no way to find out who she blackmailed."

"Actually, we do."

The dog, my daughter, my housekeeper, Mr. Coffee, and my husband spoke as one, "How?"

"The thrift shop keeps a log of all donations."

Grace frowned. "Mom, there must be hundreds of names on that list. Maybe thousands."

"True," I ceded. "But I think we could limit the time frame to the past few weeks."

"There could still be hundreds."

"We can compare those names to the people who attended last night."

A slow grin split Anarchy's face. "Mrs. Jones, have I told you that you're brilliant?"

"Not today."

He brushed a quick kiss across my lips. "You're brilliant. I need to make a few calls. I'll be in the study."

"When you're done, I'll call Libba for the guest list."

"We already have it," said Grace. "There's a copy in my room." She ran up the back stairs.

Ding, dong.

This time, Anarchy and I opened the front door.

"Zane." I held out my hands. "Have you found her?"

He shook his head. There were bags under his eyes and his skin hung loose on his frame, as if he'd spent the whole night worrying and pacing.

"Come inside." I beckoned. "What can we get you? Coffee? Tea?"

"Coffee, please," he croaked.

"Have a seat in the living room." Aside from the flower arrangements that still dotted every table and the lingering smell of alcohol and cigarette smoke, the living room was pristine.

Aggie must have stayed up half the night cleaning. "I'll be right back."

I stuck my head into the kitchen. "Aggie, may we have coffee in the living room? Also, if you have time, I'd love for you to join us."

"I'll be in shortly."

"Thank you."

I returned to the living room, where Zane rested his forearms on his knees and his head in his hands.

"No news?" I asked.

"None." Anarchy had said Dot and Zane had marital problems, but, to me, the man seemed utterly destroyed by her disappearance.

"When you arrived last night, did Dot show any interest in a car?"

He looked up. "How did you know?"

Anarchy and I exchanged a glance. "Lucky guess."

Aggie arrived with a tray, and I poured Zane a cup of coffee while she found a chair.

Zane didn't seem to notice the woman in the chartreuse kaftan. Instead, he sipped greedily.

"Which car?" I asked.

"A Mercedes." He shrugged. "There were at least fifteen Mercedes parked on your block last night. I don't know what was so special about that one, but Dot went pale and said she had to talk to you right away." He took another sip of coffee. "What did she say?"

"Not much. But I suspect she recognized the car from the crime scene."

Anarchy frowned at me. I'd said too much.

"You mean the thrift shop?"

I nodded.

"It was just a Mercedes. Nothing special."

"No bumper stickers or decals in the windows?"

"I didn't notice." He put his mug on the coffee table and stared at me with red-rimmed eyes. Worry had ground the poor man to a fine powder. "Do you think whoever killed Avery has Dot?"

Oh dear Lord. I looked to Anarchy for help.

"We're not sure, Mr. Thompson. She could have gone home with a friend."

"She wouldn't do that."

"Help us, Zane."

He shifted his gaze to me. "How?"

"What color was the Mercedes?"

"Black."

"Kansas or Missouri plates?" Living within a stone's throw of the state line, I saw as many Kansas license plates as Missouri.

He closed his eyes. "Missouri."

"Coupe or sedan?"

"Sedan."

Anarchy stood. "I'll make that call. Please ask Grace to bring me the list."

"Of course," I replied.

Anarchy crossed the front hall and disappeared into the study.

"How else can I help?" asked Zane.

I didn't know.

"Your wife is a smart woman, yes?" Aggie smoothed her kaftan over her knees.

Zane stared at her as if surprised she was in the room. "Yes. Why?"

"She wouldn't leave a party with someone she suspected of murder."

"No. Of course not."

"Perhaps she left with a friend and hasn't awakened yet. Maybe she called home this morning."

Hope brightened Zane's dull features. He stood and took a first step toward the front door. "I'll go home and check."

"Please let us know if you hear anything."

He paused and looked at me. "Please do the same."

"We will," I promised.

CHAPTER NINETEEN

We sat at a long table at the Pam Pam Room next to the window overlooking the Plaza. Gordon and Aunt Sis sat across from Anarchy and me (we had our backs to the view). My family, minus Marjorie and her husband, who'd booked an early flight, sat to our left. Anarchy's family sat to our right.

We'd lined up for the buffet, and everyone but Journey had plates filled with scrambled eggs, bacon, cinnamon rolls, biscuits and gravy, pancakes, or made-to-order omelets. Journey's plate held undressed salad and a selection of fruit.

She stabbed a blueberry with her fork as if the berry had wronged her. I couldn't help but wonder if she'd be more pleasant if she actually ate.

Oscar chewed in silence, shoveling eggs into his mouth as he scowled down the length of the table.

River chatted quietly with Aunt Sis.

Celeste and Mother took turns shooting death glares at each other.

This brunch was every bit as awful as Grace predicted.

Daddy tapped his spoon against his coffee cup and waited

until he had everyone's attention. "I couldn't let this morning pass without officially welcoming Anarchy to our family."

Aunt Sis and Gordon, who had mimosas, lifted them, ready to toast our happiness. Mother clutched her Bloody Mary and looked ill. Grace smirked.

Daddy lifted his coffee cup. "Normally I'd say something about married life being a grand adventure, but you two have enough adventure. So, I wish you quiet evenings, calm morning, and lazy weekends, all enjoyed together. To Ellison and Anarchy."

We clinked glasses and cups and drank.

At the Jones's end of the table, Celeste and Oscar had a quiet argument.

Celeste lost. She raised her herbal tea and said, "I never expected Anarchy to marry. Especially not a woman like Ellison."

My hands tightened in my lap. If she brought up my vagina, I'd cause a scene.

"Sometimes," she continued, "love is unexpected. I hope you're happy."

I forced a tight smile. "To happiness."

Anarchy stood, and I grabbed his wrist. Desperation gave me super-strength. "You can't leave me here."

He nodded toward the hostess stand. "Peters. I'll be right back."

"Hurry."

"Excuse me," Anarchy said to our families. Then he left the table and followed Peters into the broad hallway outside the restaurant.

"Ellison," said Aunt Sis. "What time does your plane leave?"

I thanked heaven for my aunt, who could make conversation out of nothing. "Four o'clock."

"Are you packed?"

"I am."

"Venice." She sighed. "I'm jealous."

"I'll take you," said Gordon. "When would you like to go?"

"This fall?" she replied. "Celeste, do you and Oscar travel?"

"Not together. Oscar likes communes, I like artist colonies."

Aunt Sis smiled politely.

Mother looked like she'd sucked a lemon.

"Ellison." Anarchy beckoned to me. "Can I borrow you for a moment?"

I stood immediately. "Excuse me."

He led me to the hallway and Peters.

"What did you find?" I asked.

"Three women made thrift shop donations and attended your reception. Jane Addison."

"Who else?"

He frowned. "Pam Ellis."

"The third woman?"

"Laura Gilchrist."

Three women I knew well. "Janes drives a Mercedes. What about the other two?"

"We're checking. It's difficult to get information from the DMV on a Sunday."

"Any luck finding Dot?

"Not yet." Peters cleared his throat and tugged at his already wrinkled collar. "Also, I'm sorry."

"For?"

"I should have told Rogan you were innocent. I'm sorry I didn't."

Peters had apologized. To me. I blinked back my surprise. "Apology accepted, Detective."

"Do you need us for anything else?" asked Anarchy.

Peters grunted.

I peeked into the restaurant, where Karma and Aunt Sis seemed to be carrying the weight of conversation. My feet refused to carry me back to the disastrous brunch. "I believe I'll stop by the powder room before I return to the table." I kissed Anarchy's cheek, walked past the closed gift shop and into the ladies' lounge, where I sank onto a stool in front of the lighted vanity.

I stared at the woman in the mirror. Ellison Jones. That would take some getting used to. Not that I minded. I smiled at my reflection. Tomorrow I'd see my reflection in an Italian mirror. If I survived this brunch.

The door swung open, and a woman entered. My heart stuttered as I recognized her in the mirror. "Laura."

Her eyes widened. "Ellison, what a surprise."

"Is it?" I stood.

She frowned. "I thought you'd be on your honeymoon."

"You didn't know I was having brunch with my family?"

"No."

Maybe Laura wasn't the killer. "I should get back to the table."

She blocked the door.

Maybe she was the killer. I tightened my hold on my handbag. "Excuse me."

She didn't budge. "We never come here. For brunch, I mean. But this morning, Charles insisted." Her chin wobbled.

Neither of us moved.

"Do you or Charles drive a Mercedes sedan?"

Her shoulders sagged. "Who else knows?"

"Anarchy and his partner." Translation: hurting me won't save you.

"It's over." She sounded almost relieved.

"You killed them?"

"Me? No!"

"Charles?"

She dissolved into tears.

"He killed Avery and Rose?"

Her hands flew to her throat. "I didn't know. I swear."

"And Lilly?"

Her mouth moved but no words came out.

"Where's Dot Thompson?"

Laura inhaled. "She was tied up in our basement."

"Was?"

"I untied her and told her to sneak out after we left for brunch."

I had to tell Anarchy. I pushed past Laura and stepped into the hallway.

Charles waited for his wife ten feet away.

Our gazes caught, and long seconds passed.

I used those seconds to pray he didn't have the gun he'd used to shoot Rose.

Charles broke our stare and ran.

I reacted without thinking and raced after him.

Charles was fast, but I was faster. When I got close, I launched myself into the air and tackled him from behind.

We crashed to the floor.

"Ellison Walford Russell Jones, what the hell are you doing?" Of course Mother would witness this.

"He killed Avery. Where's Anarchy?"

Charles was bigger than me and still struggling. Only our tangled legs kept him on the floor. His elbow drove backward and connected with my stomach.

"*Oomph!* Give up," I gasped. "You're caught."

He struggled harder, and my right hand searched for a way to hold him down. When his hair came loose in my hand, I screamed as if I'd picked up a dead rat. I threw the toupée in the air.

I didn't mean for the fake hair to hit Mother in the face. I'd swear that on a stack of Bibles.

But it did.

Mother shrieked louder than I thought possible, and Anarchy and Peters came running from the lobby.

"He did it," I yelled. "Charles is the killer."

Peters rolled his eyes, pulled out his handcuffs, and arrested Charles for three murders.

ANARCHY and I sat in the front seat of his sedan. Aggie sat in the back. She'd agreed to drive the car home from the airport.

Anarchy's hand claimed my fingers and squeezed.

I turned in my seat and glanced back at Aggie. We'd promised to fill her in during the drive.

She wore a furrow in her brow. "You were right?"

"About everything," Anarchy replied. "Charles had an affair with his law partner's daughter. They took Polaroids of, well..." One wouldn't think a tough homicide detective could blush, but Anarchy's cheeks colored.

"I get it," said Aggie. "How old was the girl?"

"Eighteen. Not criminal, but young enough to destroy Gilchrist's firm and marriage. The pictures were in an inside pocket of a sports coat Laura donated to the thrift shop."

I picked up the story. "Rose found the photos and demanded ten thousand dollars."

"So he killed her," said Aggie. "But why kill Avery?"

Anarchy's lips thinned. "Gilchrist was smart. He figured if he killed a League member, the police would focus on that murder."

"He was also lucky." No one could blame Anarchy and Peters for focusing on Avery.

"He killed a woman nearly everyone wanted dead."

"What about Lilly Frasier?" asked Aggie.

I shook my head. "She saw Charles come home covered in blood. But Lilly didn't want money. She wanted a sure entre into the country club."

Aggie nodded slowly. "So he drowned her. What did his wife know?"

"Nothing about Avery or Rose," I replied. "She wondered about Lilly. Then Dot drank too much at our reception and told Charles she'd seen his car at the thrift shop. He forced Laura to help him abduct her."

"What was he going to do with her?"

I waited for Anarchy to answer. When he remained silent, I said, "Force her to write a confession, then fake her suicide."

"What will happen to Laura Gilchrist?"

"Nothing," said Anarchy. "Her husband coerced her into kidnapping Dot. And, at the first opportunity, Laura helped Dot escape."

"And Mr. Gilchrist?"

Anarchy's lips curled in a dangerous smile. "It's a solid case. He'll be in jail for the rest of his life."

"I don't understand why the Gilchrists came to the Alameda."

"Charles spent the reception eavesdropping. He heard Grace complain about the brunch and Ellison talking about the murders. He wanted Laura to find out how much Ellison knew."

"I wasn't entirely sure Laura was innocent, and we were alone in the ladies' lounge, then Anarchy burst in." I smiled at him. "How did you know to come?"

He squeezed my hand. "Seeing Gilchrist in the hallway was too much of a coincidence."

Aggie leaned back against her seat. "I'm just glad you solved the murders before your trip."

"Me, too." Anarchy and I spoke as one.

He parked the car at the curb and popped the trunk.

Moments later, our bags disappeared with a skycap.

I hugged Aggie. "Take care of Grace."

"I will. You have a marvelous time. Send us a postcard."

I looked over her shoulder and winked at my waiting husband. "I promise."

Anarchy gave Aggie his car keys, then he took my hand in his. “Ready to go, Mrs. Jones?”

I loved hearing that name. “More than you’ll ever know.”

Holding hands, we boarded the flight for Italy and an adventurous future.

LET'S STAY IN TOUCH!

If you'd like to stay up to date with Ellison's adventures, please sign up for my newsletter! I'll keep you up-to-date on sales, releases and sneak-peeks.

ALSO BY JULIE MULHERN

The Country Club Murders

The Deep End

Guaranteed to Bleed

Clouds in My Coffee

Send in the Clowns

Watching the Detectives

Cold as Ice

Shadow Dancing

Back Stabbers

Telephone Line

Stayin' Alive

Killer Queen

Night Moves

Lyin' Eyes

The Poppy Fields Adventures

Fields' Guide to Abduction

Fields' Guide to Assassins

Fields' Guide to Voodoo

Fields' Guide to Fog

Fields' Guide to Pharaohs

Fields' Guide to Dirty Money

Fields' Guide to Smuggling

Bayou Series

Bayou Moon

Bayou Nights

CPSIA information can be obtained
at www.ICGtesting.com
Printed in the USA
BVHW040215240222
630000BV00013B/440

9 781732 755994